The Wanderer's Enduring Love

The Wanderer's Enduring Love

Marshall B. Crowder
Luz Eneida Torres

J. Kenkade
PUBLISHING®
Little Rock, Arkansas

J. Kenkade Publishing
6104 Forbing Rd
Little Rock, AR 72209
www.jkenkadepublishing.com
Facebook.com/jkenkadepublishing

J. Kenkade Publishing is a registered trademark.

Printed in the United States of America
ISBN 978-1-944486-88-4

Table of Contents

1
Arkansas

I looked at my watch and we were a full 2 hours early for our flight. Boarding wouldn't even start for another hour and a half, but Marcel had never missed a flight in his life, and he wasn't about to start now. I didn't mind. I'd gotten accustomed to being more than just a little early, we were ALWAYS super early and super organized. Knowing this, I took my time in the restroom to put on a little makeup, comb out my hair, and put back all of my belongings that the TSA had required me to take off. As I started to walk back to our table at the airport lounge, I could hear him before I could see him. His loud, boisterous laugh punctuated by a couple of hearty slaps to the knees. I swear I could hear his thick, country accent even in his laugh. My Marcel, he who never met a stranger. I could see that he'd been joined by a tall gentleman who looked to be in his early 60's, confident, smartly dressed, and thoroughly amused by whatever story Marcel was sharing. I looked at him and smiled. As Marcel passed me a drink, he introduced us. "Honey Bunches, this is Thomas. He's on his way to Cameroon to build some gas stations. Thomas, this is my wife Neida. She's from Puerto Rico by way of a lot of other places, but we met in Little Rock..." I raised my eyebrows as I took a sip of my drink and responded excitedly to Thomas, "Oh, gas stations huh? That's interesting." We went back and forth with Thomas about how long we would be there and where we'd be staying. Thomas had been there before, so he offered some travel tips for navigating the confusing streets outside of the airport and suggested some things we might enjoy while we were there. The conversation turned to couples activities and then marriage, and Thomas asked how long Marcel and I had been married. We both looked at each other and laughed, we couldn't contain our delight because that was a question that was asked of us time and time again even before we got married. We were told that the way we interacted, the way we looked at each other, and the way we regarded each other was as if we'd been married for 50 years. Marcel smiled broadly and replied, "We've only been married for a couple of months. Actually, 3 months next week. We're going on our honeymoon. We found out through DNA that we're from the same village in Cameroon, but guess how we met?" He was on the edge of his chair now, and before Thomas had a real chance to answer, Marcel leaned over toward him and said in a loud whisper that really wasn't a whisper at all, "We met online!" Then he grabbed Thomas' shoulder and continued, "...on a dating site! Can you believe that? I met the love of my life, my Honey Bunches, on the computer!" I loved the way he told the story because he was animated and looked so happy, I couldn't believe that I bought him so much joy. If we weren't already married, I'd marry him again! Thomas responded, "Golly, I would have guessed you two were married at least ten years!" He appeared just a little confused and asked, "Y'all are from the same village, so does that mean you are related?" We both said, "No!" Marcel was getting ready to explain, but Thomas stopped him. He raised his glass, made a toast, congratulated us, and said, "Now that we have time to kill waiting for our flight, you'll have to tell me all about it."

$$c_\frown$$

Whitesburg

I was raised in a small town just outside Atlanta with the overwhelming love of my parents and extended family. As an adult listening to the retelling of other people's childhood, I could see that mine was blessed. My parents were young when they had me, not even twenty years old. They wanted to make sure they were the perfect parents, and for me they were. Mama stayed home and took care of me and my sisters. Daddy dutifully provided for his family and by all accounts was very successful at it. Ours wasn't a large family, my paternal grandparents only had 2 children and my maternal grandparents had 2.

Mama grew up about 35 minutes outside of Atlanta in Rico, GA. Atlanta will be known as one of the most rapidly economical and diversified cities over the last several decades.

Growing up in a small community everyone knew or knew of each other. As I got older, I wanted to learn more about the history of the city where Mama grew up. In high school I had a Puerto Rican girlfriend named Isabel, and I shared with her how much I wanted to find out about the city and Mama's history. She called it "La Ciudad con Muchos Secretos", the city with many secrets. That's exactly what it was. Family and friends went to their graves holding onto secrets about paternity, crimes, and affairs of the heart. Sometimes to the detriment of their own families. I have asked myself "Why" over and over. Was it to protect the people they loved? Or was it more like I suspected and just a selfish act to protect themselves and their character? Whatever it was, as I've heard many times before as a child, what is done in the dark will definitely come to the light.

My mother was born at the beginning of the civil rights movement. Her brother, my uncle, worked in the fields of a local farmer, but my grandmother felt like it was interfering with his education, which she felt would determine his future, so she didn't allow him to go back to the farm. The farmer became so enraged that he drove by my grandmother's house and fired off a gunshot that struck my uncle. Fortunately, it was not fatal. My uncle recovered from his injuries, enlisted in the Army, became a highly ranked officer, and enjoyed a very successful life. After the shooting occurred, my grandmother was angry and wanted to take matters into her own hands. More than anything she wanted revenge. Everyone knew who fired the shots, but being in the Jim Crow south, nothing was done. Had my grandmother acted on her anger, she would have been seen as the aggressor, as not knowing her "place" and more than likely hung as was done often to keep us subservient. She was advised to let it go, forget about it, and keep her family. No one had gotten "seriously" injured, and it could have been much worse than it was for her. It hurt her deeply that she could not protect her son.

My grandmother, may she rest in peace, was my heart. She was the love of my life. The 10 short years that she was a part of my life were the most amazing years that I could remember. I have nothing but fond memories of my grandmother. She was a very devout, strong, and sturdy woman. She didn't have much, but what she had she would always share. Whenever I came over, she would have me pick a sunflower from her garden and some wood for her stove. Together we'd roast sunflower seeds, for me this was the best tasting treat. She'd have me go into the chicken coop to gather eggs that she'd boil for us to eat on her front porch. She made sure to always have enough money to buy my favorite ice cream at the general store, and during a time when she could barely save enough to buy herself anything new, she saved what little money she had to buy me brand new toys. Her unexpected death from lupus when I was 10 was the first death I'd experienced and the first death in my family. We knew she was sick but not that she had lupus, and in that time we didn't know that lupus would take her life. She kept the details and the severity of her illness from us. We were in total shock. How could she keep this from us? If she would have told us we could've helped her, supported her, and taken care of her. Her death left a void in my life that has never been filled. I couldn't process the loss, and to lose such an influential and loving woman like her at such a young age had me question my life, my family, and God. It affected my ability to trust in love and to love freely for fear of losing it all again. My grandmother was a God-fearing woman. She deserved to live a long and happy life. Why would God take her away from me before I was ready to let her go? I knew that I'd never be able to visit with her, and she'd never be able to be a part of my life ever again. I don't know how my life would have turned out with her in it, but I know that some of the things that occurred would have been different because of her. I didn't know how to ask for help processing my loss, and I didn't want to be a bother to Mama because she was dealing with it as well. As time moved forward I eventually did as well, never forgetting her, just moving forward with my life as she would want me to.

You can say I was born with a silver spoon in my mouth because I was the 1st grandchild for both sets of grandparents, I like to say I was born with an entrepreneurial spirit. It was while attending elementary school that I started to feel my way through life in my own way. I was the kid in the neighborhood that sold everything from bicycle reflectors to Kool-Aid. When Mama would buy potato chips, I'd divide them into small baggies and sell them for a quarter each at school. I looked for new and different ways that I could monetize everything, not because I needed money but because I enjoyed making it. If I saw a need I would find a way to fill it, and I was very good at it. I have an uncle who owned a very successful, albeit small, medical supply company. My cousin and I would often to go with him on his deliveries and as he meticulously loaded and unloaded supplies. We would sit in the back of the van and wish out loud. "I can't wait until I'm old enough to have my own business!" I said. My cousin looked at me wistfully and responded, "I can't wait until I'm old enough to get my license and run this business ourselves!" My aunt owned a very popular hair salon, Total Image Hair, that was the talk of the town. She had several stylists working for her, five women and one man. She was very open minded and forward thinking and broke barriers by hiring the first male, openly gay hairstylist in our small town, Jonathan. I'd never seen a gay person and had no knowledge of any "alternative" lifestyles or what it even meant. Jonathan was just Jonathan. We talked sports, cars, and we talked about the women that came into the salon. Everyone was anxious to be in his chair. I worked there evenings and weekends in the summers whenever I didn't have football. In the beginning I'd wash towels, sweep up hair, and as I got more responsible my aunt would let me rinse hair or help remove rollers. That was my dream job! And I loved it. I would go about my job quietly listening to the women as they talked about the men in their lives and what they did or failed to do. They talked about what they wanted from their lives and their men. They talked about what they expected (and usually never got). I felt like I was being given all the answers to what I needed to do to win any woman's heart. Being at the salon helped turn me into a great listener, a great lover, and of course it added to my charm.

$$c\rightarrow$$

Puerto Rico

Our lives in Puerto Rico were idyllic. We weren't rich but Papi was a very hard worker. He was a machinist, a baker, and a working, self-taught musician who was sought after all over the island. We lived in a modest house in the city center in Caguas with all of the modern conveniences. My father was very proud of his family, and Mami took the task of wife and mother seriously. Papi never left the house unless he was in a fresh shirt that was ironed and starched. When he got up at 4am to go bake bread she was up with him making sure he had his breakfast and hot coffee. When he got home in the evenings, we were clean and ready to have dinner with him as a family. We were all well behaved and always clean and tidy. Above all, we were loved. Their leisure-time was usually spent with us as a family. When we would go out together after dinner, we'd often hear people exclaim, "Don Lucas, que bella familia!" Tipping his hat and leading my brothers by the hand he'd respond, "Muchas gracias." The women would always fawn over me and my two sisters.

"!Hay, per que linda son, Dios las bendiga!"

"¡Y esta carita, que belleza!"

It was a life that I would have loved to live forever but it changed dramatically the day Mami received a call from my grandmother, Alejandrina, letting her know that my grandfather, Modesto, had been missing for several weeks and she was needed in New York the next day. Mami was confused, "Missing?" she asked. She had not even known that her parents had moved to the states! My grandmother didn't care too much for Mami, and by extension us, so it wasn't a surprise that they had left without telling her. Even if my grandfather wanted to, the Grandmother would not have allowed it. The Grandmother was a small yet strong woman, she had her first child at 14. She bore 11, and all of them survived by sheer grit. When I was older, she would tell me stories of how she would deliver a baby alone in the tobacco fields in the heat of the day. She would clean up the baby and wrap it up in one of her skirts and go back to tending her tobacco. She wasn't very affectionate (at least not to any of Mami's kids), and words of encouragement were viewed as a waste of time. If she liked you, she let you know it. If she didn't like you, you didn't exist. She'd waste no time on pleasantries. Although we lived in the same city, they barely spoke. At first, she complained that our house had cobwebs (it didn't), that's why she didn't visit. Then she complained that it was in a bad part of town, but it didn't stop her from visiting her friend who lived down the street. Then she stopped making excuses and just never came to visit. Even still, it came as a total shock to learn that my grandfather had been missing for days and that they'd waited so long to call Mami and let her know. All I could hear Mami say repeatedly was, ¿Como?

¿Que?

And ¿Cuando?

As the story went, my grandfather had gotten home from work at the factory and wanted to visit his adult son Americo who lived in Brooklyn. It was wintertime in New York, and my grandfather having only finished the 3rd grade didn't know how to read or write very well and having just recently arrived in New York, he knew even less in English. He knew how to get around the city by memorizing landmarks, but he wanted to take my uncle José, who was 10 years old, with him because José knew more English than he did and if necessary could translate, so it made it easy to go around town. The Grandmother shouted at him, believing that he just wanted to go out and get drunk even though my grandfather was not a heavy drinker. After grabbing my uncle by his arm and pulling him next to her, she shouted more and told my grandfather that he could go and get drunk if he wanted to, but the boy stayed home with her. After losing the debate, my grandfather, defeated and emasculated, grabbed his jacket and hat and left the apartment. And that was the last time anyone saw him. Rumors ran rampant when word got out. Some said he got lost in a snowstorm. We also heard that the Grandmother had him bumped off and then thrown in the building's incinerator. Then there was the story that he had left the Grandmother because he was fed up with her and started a new life in North or South

Carolina. No one knows for sure, but I know the Grand-mother was a horrible person, so my guess is that he left her. Mami was pregnant, and with four of us children to travel with, it would be too much. My parents decided that we would go after Mami delivered in about 4 months. Papi was working in New York and had to come back sooner than expected so he could be in Puerto Rico to tie up any loose ends and sell whatever we could to help finance the move, which at the time we had no idea it would be permanent.

We had been in Puerto Rico all of our lives, so the thought of getting in a big plane and flying across the ocean to New York was beyond anything that we could imagine. I was too young to care, but my brothers and sisters weren't. Hiram and Rosa were both excited and eager to go. They would entertain each other for hours on end with wild stories and ideas of what New York was like. In their childish minds we'd be going to a faraway and magical place where the buildings were a million feet tall and the fluffy snow that fell from the sky tasted like coconut. Rosa was going to ask Papi to buy her a quilted coat made of candy and gum pieces, and of course she would share with us because the candy pieces would grow back. Angel even at his young age was more solemn and ambivalent at the thought of leaving. He didn't want to go, he begged to stay with Mr. Villa who owned the corner store down the street. Mr. Villa was one of Angel's favorite people. He stopped and visited with Mr. Villa every day after school and ate all the mangoes he could pick from the tree in the back. He wanted to stay and play with the lizards that he caught in our backyard.

He and Hiram would let the lizards bite their ear lobes and let them hang like earrings. He didn't want to leave his school and his friends. He cried and was inconsolable when he didn't know where we'd live. Mami had to remind him that we would all be together so he should not worry. Days later, when Angel resigned himself to the fact that he was leaving he looked all over for a jar. When he couldn't find one to his liking, he ran to Mami and asked her, "¿Mami, tu tiene un pote?" Do you have a jar?

Mami looked at him and asked, a jar? What do you need a jar for?

"¿Pa que tu quieres un pote?"

Exasperated, Angel kept looking and when he couldn't find one, he ran out the door to the corner store and he asked Mr. Villa,

"¿Don Villa usted tiene un pote?" Do you have a jar?"

Mr. Villa looked at him puzzled and said what do you need a jar for?

"¿Oye, pa que tu quiere up pote?"

Shoving his hands deep into his pockets and shrugging his small shoulders he looked up at Mr. Villa, and with tears in his eyes he responded, "Pa llevar me un poquito de Puerto Rico." To make sure that I can take a little of Puerto Rico with me. Understanding the urgency, Mr. Villa looked on the top shelf and carefully lowered several jars for Angel to inspect.

"Toma M'ijo, coje el que te guste," he said, and Angel wiped the tears from his eyes and grabbed one and ran back home. As he ran in, he stopped in the kitchen and picked up a spoon from the sink. When he reached a shady corner in the back yard he got on his knees and began spooning fresh dirt into the jar. There in the backyard he filled it with fresh Puerto Rican dirt.

C↷

New York

The air smelled faintly of floor cleaner. Mami was talking to me, but her words sounded muffled and far away even though I was standing right next to her. Hiram sat on a bench playing with a toy car. Angel sat next to him cradling the jar of dirt that he brought with him all the way from home. My hands were beginning to sweat, I looked at them and then down at my patent leather shoes. They were so shiny I could see the lights of the ceiling reflecting off of them. The baggage claim seemed so vast and strange with so many people huddled around waiting. I shifted my weight again and again and tried to focus on holding the straps of my mother's purse. I felt her hand on my head, and I looked at her with pleading eyes as I tried not to pee my pants. I don't remember how long we'd been traveling or where we were going, all I knew was that I had to pee and nothing else mattered. Mami called Hiram over from the bench where he'd been sitting quietly and passed him the baby. "Coje la beba en lo que llevo a Neida al bano," she said while she put Judy in his arms. Relieved and with a new burst of energy, I skipped along beside her as we headed to the restroom. She lifted me up onto the commode and kissed my cheek. I could smell the faint scent of Chanel No. 5 on her neck. No matter where Mami was going, to the market, school, church, or the doctor's office, she always made sure she smelled nice by dabbing a little bit of perfume behind her ears and on her wrist. Smelling good was a vice that Mami always kept throughout her whole life. Mami's style was very cosmopolitan, after all, she'd been to San Juan and Ponce. I would often overhear her speaking with her girlfriends about the styles and fashion of Jackie Kennedy, Marilyn Monroe, and the current Miss Puerto Rico 1967, beauty queen and actress, Ivonne Coll. Mami was a seamstress, and she sewed all of our clothes, so she had an easy time of duplicating whatever style of dress was in fashion for us and for herself.

She tapped my fleshy thigh and asked,

"Ya terminaste?" she asked as she began to lift me down from the commode.

I nodded and grabbed some toilet paper, balled it up, and gave it to her to wipe, but she had already wiped me. I put the ball in my pocket and tried to help her pull up my underwear. Smoothing my sweater, I followed her to the sink so she could wash my hands with the pink powdered soap she pushed out of the dispenser attached to the wall. Relieved and refreshed, we went back out to the baggage claim to wait for Papi.

2

Cameroon
Marcelo & Lusamba

Marcelo was a strong young man from a long bloodline of strong and proud men and women of Dizangue, a village in the Littoral province of Cameroon along the Sanaga River. He was the eldest of three children. He was a great hunter and leader. Marcelo would soon be the head of his own family once he took a bride. His bride to be was a beautiful young lady named Lusamba with hypnotic brown eyes, full cheeks, and lips as red as the Palisota barteri that cover the forest floor. Her hair was to her calves, long, wavy, and brown, and her skin was fresh like the tall ayous trees. She was the youngest of three daughters. Her sisters lived in the village with their families as well. Her parents were the healers and looked after the sick and injured, and her mother attended to the births in the village. When Lusamba wasn't doing her chores, you could find her at the edge of the forest being one with nature. He enjoyed watching her and her full hips and thighs as they swayed with every step she took. He was so in love with this young lady, not just for her overwhelming beauty, but for her spirit was as of an angel from the heavens. She made him laugh with her simple observations and sense of humor. She had a sincere and genuine way about her. He wanted to hold on to her forever.

The rainy season was soon to begin and was cause for celebration for all of the nearby villages. They were preparing for a celebration of love and appreciation for the gift of rain seen as a blessing to the earth, their bodies, and their souls. Lusamba had been feeling ill at ease for most of the morning, not knowing if it was the excitement of tomorrow's activities or some more serious indication of impending danger, so she just brushed it off. The excitement of getting ready for the celebration of the spring season was making her head spin. The whole village was abuzz with activity. They were busy with one task or another, weaving baskets to catch rainwater, the children were practicing their songs and dancing and preparing for what would be tomorrow. Throughout the course of the day, all the preparations were done in frenzied excitement. In the next village over there was also quite a stir. Marcelo lived there, and he was helping out with most of the men's work like killing and butchering pigs and goats that would feed most of the village for the ceremonies. Their villagers would be marching with their drums down in a procession at sunrise to mark the beginning of the rainy season. He was working fast and hard so he'd have time to visit with Lusamba. He knew it was getting late. As soon as he was finished, he started towards her village. He couldn't wait to see her. His bare feet did not move fast enough. As it grew dark, she looked up at the moonless night. She heard him calling from behind a bohio and ran to him. Holding him tightly she looked up at him and smiled. It was hard for her to put into words how much she loved him. They were from different villages, but they'd found ways to be together. They understood each other, and soon they'd be together as husband and wife. They laid on the bare grass holding each other, looking up, and counting the stars that shone so brightly. He pointed out the brightest ones and said, "See there? That star there is you. The bright one next to it that is me." He continued to explain, "Out of all the many stars in the sky those two are together like us, and they will be forever." He kissed her softly and held her tight. They felt the light rain as it started to fall on their bodies and quickly got up. Kissing her forehead and holding her hands with the promise to see each other on the next day, they parted ways. Marcelo was giddy with excitement. He could not wait for the day to ask for her to be his wife. Thoughts of her and their life together were running through his mind as he made his way back to his village when suddenly he heard a noise in the brush that made him stop. He walked away, looking back to get one last glimpse of her in the moonlight, not ever thinking this would be the last time he would see his future wife.

He walked on this same path many times leaving their favorite place. By now the rain was coming down so heavily it obstructed his view and sense of direction. Unknowingly, he veered off the usual path, and out of nowhere he felt something cover his entire body. He was disoriented, tangled, and wet. Marcelo fought his invisible attacker with every breath he had to give before transcending into darkness. He knew he had passed out because he woke up after what appeared to be several hours later shackled to villagers he knew and several ones he had never seen and was left wondering what his destiny would be. Would he be killed? Was he being taken as a prisoner? He could not explain it. His village was not at war with any other village. Would he ever see his true love ever again? Would he ever get back home to the life he once knew and loved?

Lusamba woke up early the next morning way before dawn since the festivities would start promptly at sunrise. There was a lot of commotion happening and she could hear people screaming and crying more than the usual commotion for the rain festival. She rushed out to the center of the village to see that a lot of her neighbors and friends were crying and screaming. She didn't know why, but she saw some women from the neighboring village where Marcelo was from and they too were crying and screaming. The elders were frantically trying to get the situation under control. Lusamba looked from one woman to the next, seeing the same look of anguish and despair. She walked over to one of the women she knew and asked, "What is going on?" The distraught woman cried as she explained, "Sometime in the middle of the night strangers came into the village and took my husband." Lusamba opened her eyes wide with disbelief. "What do you mean, who took him, and took him where?" she asked, feeling the sting of tears in the back of her eyes and a lump begin to form in her throat. Crying, the woman responded, "I don't know, I don't know!"

Suddenly it all sank in. She felt the life leave her body; she was numb. She brought her hands up to her chest trying to slow down the fast beating of her heart. She ran out to the edge of the village where just hours ago she was with him, but no one was there. Then she ran to the place where all the celebrations were going to be held, no one there. She ran to where they would be preparing the meals. She saw that the pigs were wrapped in banana leaves and the goats were already in a cooking pit, but the fires hadn't been started. She ran to the entrance and saw that the costumes, instruments, and headwear all laid bare. She could find no one. It wasn't long before the village elders were able to piece together what had happened and conducted a full headcount of all the villagers. Marcelo's village had lost 3 young girls and 13 young men, including Marcelo. Lusamba's village had lost 12 men, 7 women, and 4 children. Devastated, Lusamba fell down to her knees and began to scream. She heard the elders solemnly issuing instructions to the villagers and words of encouragement to those families that had been affected while prompting everyone to remember the season, but she couldn't believe it. At that moment she wanted to be with Marcelo, even if it meant she was snatched with him, at least they'd be together and she wouldn't have to deal with the unbearable heartache on her own.

He heard the voices of his captors as they were yelling orders, but no one could understand. Marcelo was in pain from the top of his head to the soles of his feet. He could tell they were being counted as they were led up a gangway. His hands were still bound, and he had to take awkward small steps since his ankles were in heavy chains, so he was pushed and pulled in whatever direction they needed to go. The men were all loaded onto a big boat. Marcelo was suddenly very scared. This was a boat bigger than any boat he'd ever seen before. None of them knew where they were being taken, and their questions were met with cracks of the whips or slaps to the head and body. Below deck reality set in. He knew that a lot of his tribesmen had been taken, but he was not prepared for what he saw. It was as if his whole village and every other village had been taken and put here, row after row of men, all of them in shackles and all with the same look of desolation on their faces. Other than the sound of the shackles and the constant grunts and moans of pain and discomfort, there was complete and utter silence. They were packed into the boat so tightly that they could barely move. They laid side by side and end to end with no room to move and nowhere to relieve themselves for days. They sailed this way, malnourished and mistreated and dying for weeks and months.

Marcelo survived the treacherous trip to the new world, but just barely. He had no concept of time as each agonizing day melded into the next. At home he loved the water, water meant life. During the end of the rainy season it bought everything back to life. Just standing at the riverbank listening to the sound of the rushing water calmed him. Here on the ship, the water meant death. Standing on the deck, in every direction all you could see was water. He grew to hate the sight of it. Even drinking it caused death. Some of the captured plunged to their deaths once the reality of their situation sunk in. On this disgusting ship everything repulsed him. The first days he was overcome with so much sickness that he could barely stand. The air below deck was foul, thick with the stench of urine and feces. It was not unusual for them to start wrenching in chorus as they were packed so tightly there was no way to avoid getting soiled or spat on. Some days they were taken to the deck of the ship to "exercise", but that ended up being just a shuffle to and fro. Marcelo used this opportunity to encourage the men to remain strong and sang songs in their language urging them to do so. A bath consisted of buckets of sea water being thrown on them, the saltwater exacerbating any cuts or bruises already on their bodies. Meals, if they could be called that, were likewise thrown as if they were animals. You would think that nightfall would bring respite, but the nighttime hours were just as agonizing. Laying shackled side by side caused horrible lesions to form all over their bodies. And the dawning of the day only bought more misery as those that perished during the night were callously and unceremoniously thrown overboard.

Marcelo stayed strong, and even through his bouts with sickness he remained physically, spiritually, and mentally strong. Although they were all from different tribes and villages, they were all captives and they formed a bond. He tried to keep their spirits up and encourage the others, "Once we get to where we are going, we can escape!" He tried to be optimistic even though there was no way he could anticipate the horrors that were in store for them. He urged them to keep their minds keen by learning of each other's families and singing songs. They attempted to learn their captor's language by deciphering what few words were yelled at them. They talked of mutiny and of jumping into the sea and hoping their gods would guide them back home. Cleanliness of the ship, crew, or themselves seemed to be out of the question. Everyone was dirty, everyone smelled bad, and everyone was sick at one time or another. It was a wonder that anyone survived the journey as enduring it was a feat in and of itself. Marcelo was shackled to another man, so every step, every breath, and every shift of the body was labored. While everyone around him succumbed to illness and even death, Marcelo believed he willed himself not to get sick, and just as he thought that he would not be able to survive one more day they reached landfall.

They knew they had reached their destination by all the commotion around them. Marcelo made a mental note to memorize every inch of their new location, as he was determined to plan an escape. After so many days at sea, they were happy to be at their destination even though they had no idea where they were. They were all tired of being scared, and those that had survived the journey and all of the ills that came along with it were weak and weary. Even at dusk the dock was a flurry of activity. They were doused in water and given rags to wear before being dragged out of the ship. They docked in Georgia, and what they saw was foreign to him. There were many people everywhere. They were led into a warehouse where they were put on makeshift platforms where strangers were allowed to grope their bodies and force their mouths open to examine their teeth. All he could do was snatch his face out of their hands. A lot of them were told to hop around in what Marcelo could think of as a test of their agility. He knew they were asking questions of them, but they could not understand. Marcelo tried his best to keep everyone calm. He assured them that there would be an opportunity for them to escape, they just needed to wait. They endured this treatment throughout the night and then early the next morning they were paraded in front of a different, more aggressive group of spectators. Marcelo was filled with anxiety and fear as he saw his fellow tribesmen one after the other being taken away, still in their shackles. He had to think of something quickly, but what? He didn't have the luxury of time, he knew if he waited he would never see his friends again. He felt an increasing urge to fight his captors and kill as many oppressors as he could, but thoughts of getting back home and to Lusamba held him back. He could not risk dying before he got back to his love. He knew he had to wait. He had to prevail. Just as he memorized his location, he memorized his tribesmen's purchasers and whatever details he could grasp. His friend Ubembo was purchased by a man named Bowen, and he noticed that he walked with a stick. He closed his eyes and silently practiced saying the name several times-- Bowen, Bowen. Kunle, who had been shackled to him, was purchased by a man named Daniel who had a bushy white beard. Determined, he made sure to commit to memory as much as he could about all 12 that were taken from his village. They were etched in his mind. He made a commitment to himself that he would get them back to their home and that he would get back to Lusamba. With no time to share his plan with any of the others, all he could do was shout "Kumbuka, Kumbuka! --Remember!" as each was taken away.

Lusamba & Elias

Two years had passed, and she had still not gotten over the devastation of losing Marcelo. Everyone told her in time the pain would go away. She wished it were true, but it was not. The pain was still there. She had stopped waiting for him to suddenly appear and wake her from this terrible nightmare. She knew, as everyone else in the village knew that they were all taken violently and inhumanely. So suddenly and without regard by someone motivated by pure greed. Yanked mercilessly from their homes, their friends, their families, and the only lives they had ever known. Taken miles and miles away across oceans and oceans to never be seen or heard from again. She was filled with questions that no one could answer. The days ran into each other as she let herself sink into her pain. A day did not go by that he wasn't on her mind and in her heart. Everywhere she looked she could see things that brought back the thought of Marcelo.

When she awoke the smell of the morning air reminded her that another day had come, and he was still gone. When she went to collect water she was reminded of how he loved to make her chores easier by carrying her full baskets for her. When she sat down to eat all she could think of was how Marcelo would joke that he was so good at butchering a goat that he would have it cleaned and hanging even before the goat realized it was dead. She cried a million tears at night as she looked up at the sky and saw the stars, remembering the pair he pointed out to her. Was he looking at the same stars? Was he hungry or cold? Was he hurt? Was he thinking of her? Was he alive? The last was a thought that only came to her on the worst of days when she herself wished she were dead. She knew that the pain of losing Marcelo would be a part of her life forever, and as she had for the last 2 years, she would cry herself to sleep.

Everyone urged her to move past her hurt, to put this terrible time behind her. She was young and had her whole life to live. "Enough is enough, Lusamba!" her mother said one day as they were drying herbs. "You've got to let the past go and live your life!" Lusamba looked at her as tears welled up in her eyes. She looked at her mother in disbelief. She didn't expect her to know how she felt, but she at least expected her to let her grieve. She became angry and yelled, "How can I live when my life WAS Marcelo? Without him I have NO life!" She left her herbs and ran away. No one understood what she and Marcelo had. He was not just her intended, he was her friend and her future. She could not see and didn't want to have a future without him. She awoke one morning filled with melancholy and angry that death had not come for her yet again. Realizing that she could not continue to mourn Marcelo, she reluctantly decided to accept the fact that he'd never return to her. Wherever he was, whether in spirit or alive, he would not like for her to be wasting her days.

With a newfound resolve Lusamba eased back into her normal routine. It was far from normal, but she had to try her best to live a life after Marcelo. She slowly rejoined her community, which seemed to be thriving, and they were glad to have her. Most of the women knew exactly what she had gone through, as they had been robbed of a loved one themselves. She felt good because she knew they understood her. They did their best to include her even on the days that were the hardest for them. There were still ceremonies that had to be held to commemorate the betrothed, new births, rites of passage, and passings. She saw that life did not stop because of her suffering.

It was difficult for her to start again, but she did. Slowly and deliberately, she awoke early and began her day. She did her chores after everyone else was finished so she wouldn't have to talk to anyone. She accompanied her mother to visit the sick because then she didn't have to talk. She bathed at night in the river when she could stare at the moonlit sky and find the stars that Marcelo pointed out to her so many times. She ate her meals by herself until one day she saw him come from his hut and sit beside her.

"Hello Lusamba," he said before he unrolled his mat and sat next to her.

"Hello Elias," she responded blandly and continued to eat.

She knew Elias, they'd been friends and she liked the security of having someone sit with her but also give her the space she needed. They sat and ate in familiar silence. When he finished his lunch, he picked up his belongings, rolled up his mat, and before walking away he said, "Bye Lusamba."

"Bye Elias."

She kept looking in his direction long after he was out of view. He was a strange one she thought and smiled.

Elias was tall, lean, and lithe. He was soft spoken and observant. His parents were well respected and contributed very much to their village. His father was a great fisherman and hunter and someone Elias wanted to emulate. He had dedicated his time to learning and practicing with him. The villagers would often say that his father could catch fish with his bare hands. That he would just speak the name of any beast to his spear and it would be guided to it with one throw, like magic. Any beast he set his sights on was his. His mother was a weaver, a skill that was passed down from her mother. Baskets woven so tightly that you would not lose even a single drop of water. Mats of all sizes that were so comfortable you would think you were sitting or lying on a cloud. Their families had known each other, and they approved of her as his wife. Lusamba spent most of her times with Marcelo, and he would usually see them together. Elias knew like everyone else that one day they would be betrothed. At the time he was pleased that she had Marcelo and when he was captured, he hurt for her. He wanted to be there to comfort her, but he didn't know what to say.

The night the villagers were taken was a disastrous night for everyone. Elias felt his love for hunting kept him from being caught, and he was never more grateful.

He had gone to his bohio to gather some of the spears which he had just sharpened for a demonstration he was to perform during the next days' ceremonies. Had it not been for that, he would have been easy prey out in the dark night. The thought of that night paralyzed him and made him fearful. His father had been instrumental in easing him back into his routine. He told him that the night their villages were preyed upon was not by accident. Just like he trained to be a hunter of beast, there are those that train to be hunters of men. In order for him to survive, he would need to be keen and think like both hunter and prey and always remain a step ahead. He believed this to be true, so he threw himself into intense skills training so he'd never be caught by surprise again.

Lusamba continued to slowly come out of her shell, and Elias kept coming around. Every time he saw her by herself eating quietly, he would come undo his mat, sit down, and keep her company, often without saying a word. She would just look at him, chuckle and say, "Hi Elias, how are you today?" very exaggeratedly so he would know it was okay to talk to her. She didn't know that he had a million things to talk to her about and a million questions he wanted to ask, but he knew that it had to be on her terms so he waited until she asked. They were sitting down eating their lunch in silence, and Elias dared to ask if he could join her at the river that afternoon. She was surprised and said nonchalantly, "Sure, you can walk with me." So after lunch, instead of rolling up his mat, he left it where it was and grabbed her water baskets for her and they headed towards the river. In silence.

At the river Elias grabbed the baskets from her while she spoke with some of the other women, filled them, and when she was ready he carried them back toward the village. All in silence. They continued this way for the next couple of weeks. They had a mutual understanding, she allowed him to sit with her at lunch, and he would accompany her to the river. He wouldn't push her to talk, and he would ask for no more. Then one day it all changed. She was waiting for Elias to come by for lunch, she unrolled his mat closer to hers in anticipation and poured his water, but he didn't appear. She found it odd, but she brushed it off. She ate her lunch by herself and afterwards was making her way down to the river when she heard someone calling after her. "Lusamba!" he called.

"Lusamba, wait!" She looked back. When she realized it was Elias she stopped. She was happy to see him, and she didn't acknowledge that her heart actually skipped a beat. As he took her baskets out of her hands, he went on to explain that one of his younger brothers had cut his hand while they were sharpening spears, and he had to tend to him in his hut and wait for their parents to arrive so he could explain what happened. She was relieved. From that moment on they were together for most of the time. She waited for him during lunch, and together they went to the river to collect water, and together they walked back. He walked with her when she collected her herbs, and she sat with him as he sharpened his spears. They talked about everything. They reminisced about their younger days. They talked about how they felt about the snatchings. They talked about their hopes for the future and how he felt about her. He didn't expect her to be in love with him, but he loved her, and he promised that he would make her happy. She grew to love Elias and although she secretly knew that no one could compare to Marcelo, she wanted so much to be happy. Months went by and she finally conceded to let Elias officially court her.

They got married and had 3 children of their own. She could admit at least to herself that she did love him, but not like she loved Marcelo. She silently compared everything they did to what she and Marcelo did until the children came. She could only imagine how great of a father Marcelo would be and wondered if he had met someone and fallen in love. She could not deny that Elias loved his children. With the arrival of each of their children she saw his love grow. He knew they were their future, and he did all he could to nurture them. He was tender, caring, and gentle. He took them with him whenever he could, always eager to teach them new things and happy to see the world through their curious eyes. He was a great father and a great provider.

One particular morning she felt a general uneasiness since the moment she woke up, and she couldn't shake it. It was exactly how she felt when the men of the village were snatched so long ago. She felt chills run down her spine and thought something might be wrong with the children and hurriedly sought them out. She felt relief when she saw that the youngest one was asleep on a mat. From where she was standing, she saw that the others were outside playing, and Elias was tending to some livestock right next to them. She could almost see the whole village from her vantage point. She looked a little beyond her children, and she saw some strange men pouring into the village. "That was odd," she thought. She'd never seen these men before. But sooner than she could really understand what was happening, she saw Elias as he dropped his staff, roughly grabbed their children, and began to run toward her with each of the kids hanging on his side. The strange men were on some kind of cart and quickly advanced and tore him away from the children. Lusamba looked in horror from afar. Her eyes big and wide, filled with confusion, and then narrowed in anger. She saw as one man grabbed Elias and threw him onto the cart, another man came out of nowhere and knocked him on the head to subdue him and quickly tied him to the cart. Another one came from the other direction and grabbed each child and threw them in the wagon along with Elias.

Lusamba was watching it all in shock and disbelief. This could not be happening again! She let out a scream, and suddenly as if she had been electrified, she started running toward the cart. She ran as fast as she could toward her abductors with the intention of fighting them and getting her family away, but as she got to them, she felt herself being lifted off the ground. She flailed and kicked vigorously in an attempt to get loose. The man lifted her, she grabbed a handful of his hair and started slapping him. He lifted his hands in defense and grabbed both her hands and threw her on to the cart. She grunted in pain and got up and jumped off the cart and onto the back of another one of their assailants. She held on and tried to gouge his eyes out. He called out in pain for another man to come grab her and held her arms while she was quickly tied to the wagon as well. She fell in a heap, tired and defeated. She quickly looked around for her children. She found them huddled close to Elias who was just coming to. She saw more of her villagers being grabbed and loaded into the cart. One of the men went into her hut and came out with the sleeping child. She was horrified! How could this be happening again? She struggled to get closer to her family, but her ropes would not allow much movement. The children weren't tied up, and she called them over to her so she could examine them to see if they were hurt. Thankfully they were not. She heard the men speaking to each other as they loaded villager after villager into the cart with them. They were her friends and neighbors. She could see the fear in their eyes, and they saw the same in hers. She repeatedly asked "Who were these men? Where and why were they being taken?" Then she felt the full cart yanked forward as they started to leave the village.

The sun was high in the sky when they reached the beach. They were unloaded from the cart and loaded into a vessel bigger than she'd ever seen before. Lusamba's ropes were removed, and she tried to rub away the pain as she tried to assess the situation. She saw plenty of familiar faces, but they were all in the same position as she, paralyzed with fear. There was so much commotion everywhere, the men yelling in a language she didn't understand, the children weren't shackled, but they were crying and clinging to their parents. The men for their part were surprisingly quiet for fear that they'd be stuck with whatever weapon their captors were wielding. Elias had been shackled to another man, his left wrist and ankle to the other man's right wrist and ankle. All the men where shackled this way as they were boarded into the ship. Her mind was racing. She felt the fear and anxiety and dread that Marcelo must've felt years before and knew that she could not let her family board that ship! She felt that if they got on that ship it would be the end of their lives. She had to do something, but what? She looked at Elias and the other men as she was walking up the gang plank with the women and children filing in beside them. The children in their nervousness were crying and running back and forth from Lusamba to Elias. Lusamba made it to the top and was overwhelmed with such a deep sense of despair that she was afraid she'd faint. She looked at Elias, he too had a look of fright and despair in his eyes. He could not utter a word. He finally looked at her. She saw his muscles tense as sweat and tears fell from his face. She looked back and she could see the emotion in his eyes as he was motioning for her to leave. She didn't want to leave him and her children. She decided she'd rather be with him than to risk dying as she jumped ship. Her heart was racing, and she struggled to catch her breath. Scared and blinded by the tears that welled up in her eyes, she quickly surveyed the ship.

Everyone was in the front trying to make order out of the chaos that was created. There was no one around the side where cargo boxes had been loaded. She visualized an exit. She looked back for Elias and the children and saw him. "GO!" He mouthed a single word, full of force, telling her to jump before they pulled up anchor. Her trembling lips mouthed back "No" and softly pleaded with him. Reluctantly she turned and ran to the edge of the ship. She looked back longingly and before anyone could have a chance to stop her, she jumped. The shipmates saw her and tried to run after her, but there were too many bodies in their path. They yelled orders for them to move, but no one could understand and therefore stayed where they were, effectively blocking the way and giving Lusamba more time to flee. They heard who they assumed was the captain yell, "Dejala!" for them to leave her. He explained that she had probably broken her neck with the sharp rocks since they were so close to the beach. She hit the water hard and was stunned for a moment and floated until she was able to tread water and was able to make it back across to the opposite side of the ship. Exhausted, terrified, and traumatized, she laid on the beach until she was awakened by a woman who was doing her morning chores collecting driftwood.

Lusamba was battered and fatigued. The woman could see that she was in need of care and decided to take her to her village and nurse her back to health. When she was well enough, she explained how she lost her first love and now Elias and her children, she had no one. The woman understood. She'd heard how some tribes took prisoners and sold them to strangers from foreign lands for powerful weapons. These men and women were never to be seen from again. Lusamba wanted to be alone with her pain. In the days that followed she regained her strength and decided that this would be the last time she'd ever be in such a vulnerable position. She didn't want to go back home. Even if she did nothing would ever be the same for her. Marcelo was gone, Elias was gone and her sweet, beautiful children were gone. There was nothing left for her at the village except terrible memories. She had to be alone until her heart stopped hurting. She had no idea where she was going and she didn't care, but she would live her life on her own, by herself, so her heart would never be broken again.

$$\backsim$$

Elias- New World

Elias had no idea why they were taken or where they were going. He relived the moments of their capture every waking moment. None of it made sense to him. It was as if they were being systemically picked out of the village. He thought his senses were keen, he thought he'd be able to protect Lusamba, but he was wrong. He was ill-prepared for the stealth and determination of their captors. When he saw an opportunity for her to be free, he didn't hesitate. He could never know the horrors that he would be subjected to, but he knew that whatever it was he didn't want it for Lusamba. She had already been through too much. After many weeks on board the ship and just as many of being sick, abused, uncomfortable, and nearly half-dead Elias and the rest who survived the horrific journey finally made it to Puerto Rico. Luckily, Elias and the children were sold, along with a woman, Jovita, that they got close to on their journey. She saw Lusamba jump off the ship and served as the children's foster mother. She tended to them as much as she could when they were sick, which was often, and held them when they cried for their mother who they believed had died. They were sold as a unit to a Spanish Diplomat, Felipe Andres Torres Castillo, who owned a plantation with sugar and tobacco fields. Elias became the servant of this diplomat, Don Felipe. During this time there was a lot of political unrest in Puerto Rico, and one day while they were surveying the plantation, Don Felipe asked Elias, "What political party to do belong to?" Elias thought for a moment, not wanting to say the wrong thing, then proudly responded, "Maestro, of course, I belong to whatever party you belong to." Angered, Don Felipe responded inflamed, "Ah, you think so much of yourself that you would even belong to a political party!"

Elias was in shock; he couldn't understand what had angered him so much. He began to apologize as he attempted to retreat, but he was grabbed by his neck and thrown in the utility room. After several hours Don Felipe came back with a machete. Before Elias could even protest, he was tied to a table with his hands outstretched and with one swift motion Don Felipe cut off his hand. Without a second thought and even less compassion, he quickly cut off the other and hollered for Elias' wife to come tend to her husband. At the time in Puerto Rico slaves were allowed to buy their freedom from their masters if they were no longer of use. Even though he had cut off both his hands, rather than sell Elias his freedom, he packed him up and sent him far away from his family to the Canary Islands. Elias never returned to Puerto Rico or saw his family ever again.

C~

We had been traveling for some time. With nowhere to go, Thomas was a captive audience. He remained eager to hear about the dangers that Marcelo and Elias went through. Marcel and I would go back and forth explaining the story in great detail to help him understand. His major concern was that we were related. I assured him we weren't. We had moved from the airport bar to the gate and were sitting with Thomas waiting for our turn to board. He was a great listener and was very animated. He asked open-ended questions about Lusamba and Marcelo and told us he genuinely felt bad for them. He was on the edge of his seat as Marcel retold the last time they got snatched. We were interrupted by our flight attendant on the loudspeaker announcing that our flight was ready to board. Thomas asked Marcel what seats we were sitting in and if he minded if he switched his seat to be next to us. Marcel winked at me, smiled, and responded, "No, brother we don't mind that at all." And he showed him our boarding passes. Thomas got up; his section was boarding first. He grabbed his carry-on and slowly disappeared into the fuselage.

I looked around to make sure I had all my bags then sat back and waited for our section to board. Marcel got up to throw away some trash and made a detour at the counter where he stopped to talk to one of the flight attendants. I could see him flashing his smile and pointing at me. Whatever he was saying had her thoroughly amused.

He walked back to me and as he sat down he said, "Every-body loves us Honey Bunches!" That flight attendant said she just caught the tail end of the story and was anxious to hear more! I kissed him and said, "How can they not love us? We're adorable!" Another section got up to be seated. We waited for a couple of sections before ours got called and we made our way in. Just as Marcel was putting my bag in the overhead compartment, I saw that same flight attendant come up to us and ask us to follow her. I was puzzled, especially when she told him to bring our stuff. To my surprise, as we were walking behind her, she told us that we had been upgraded to 1st class with Thomas. The flight attendant led us to our row, and there was a casually dressed young man who was already sitting in the window seat. Thomas approached him and politely asked him if he'd mind switching seats with him so he could sit next to his friends. The young man didn't hesitate as he got up and reached for his carry-on and quickly moved up to his new seat. I saw the accomplished look on Thomas' face and smiled. He waited for us to store our belongings and take our seats: me in the window, Marcel next to him in the middle seat, and his seat in the aisle. When we got buckled in, he looked at Marcel and said alright, let's get right to it.

He asked, "You mean to tell me that poor girl, your great great great granny got her man snatched up twice?" Marcel was happy to get him some understanding said, "No, listen to me now...She was SUPPOSED to marry the 1st guy who was snatched, Marcelo. That was her world, her first true love, and the one she was betrothed. The 2nd guy, Elias, was a childhood friend who she grew to love and had a family with. The whole family got snatched up together and were on the slave ship and when he saw the anguish in her eyes, he told her to go be free. Because the men were shackled, but the women and children weren't! He knew that was going to be her only opportunity to flee, and he encouraged her to leave. He didn't know what was waiting for him at the other side of the journey, but he felt in his spirit that she needed to stay." Thomas lowered his head in sadness said, "Aww man, that kinda brings tears to my eyes brother!"

"I know it, she went through a lot."

"But Elias, Daggum it! What do we know about him?

We went on to explain that once he was shipped to the Canary Islands, we lost contact. For all we knew he started a whole new family there. I hoped that was true. Because that thought of my great great grandfather dying lonely with his arms chopped off was too much sadness to bear. Thomas said, "At least Marcelo was lucky and kept his hands in America" One could argue that Elias was the lucky one, who although maimed, didn't have to endure the brutality of slavery in the US. I said, "I don't know if he was lucky," but we do know that once Marcelo reached Savanah and was sold, he tried all he could to get back to Cameroon. We went on to explain more of the lineage and Thomas interjected with the appropriate exasperation and disbelief. He was anxious to hear more of our fascinating story and urged us to continue.

"Okay, go on. What happened next?"

3

Georgia
Marcel High School

Starting high school for me was surreal. For the first time I had a smorgasbord of girls right out of my dreams at every turn. I had so many to choose from, I knew I had to have a strategy that would allow me to enjoy the lovely ladies I wanted in high school. I knew that I wanted to join the football and the baseball teams and maybe even track. I had a car and a job at the salon and the Piggly Wiggly, so I was gaining my independence by leaps and bounds. My senior year at Crestview High School was great for me. My best friend David and I were inseparable. We were lucky enough to have known each other since elementary school, and now in high school instantly we had our own clique. I was an ok student, so that kept my parents off my back. I was on the football team, teachers loved me, the guys all wanted to be my friend, and the girls were always chasing after me. Being confident, fair skinned, and handsome with curly dark hair in the 90's definitely contributed to my popularity. High school helped me hone my social skills. There wasn't a conflict I could not talk my way out of. If my friends had a conflict, they would call on me to work it out for them. I had the world on a string, and I couldn't be happier. After school I made my way to the beauty salon as I usually did.

Today there were more cars than usual in the parking lot, but I didn't expect what I walked into. The place was packed! I went over to the sinks and stepped around and through some ladies until I reached my aunt who looked frantic at the end of the hall. I asked her, "What's going on today that it's so busy?" She said that Susie, Wendy, and Jonathan had called in because they had the flu! Wow, that was her whole staff for the day! Golly, I said, and then I asked her, "What can I do to help?" She asked me if I knew how to wash hair. I looked at her sideways with a look of confidence and I said, "Don't worry Auntie, I got this." I yelled out in my strongest, sexiest voice, "Ladies, ladies, I apologize for the inconvenience. I know you've been here a long time, but I'm here to help." With that I asked, "Who's next for a wash?" All the ladies stood up raising their hands as if they were at an auction house. I picked out the first three ladies from the crowd to get me started. "Alright, you with the Pretty Brown Eyes. Your love, you love me in the right place." I said, quoting a popular song that made everyone laugh. Then I pointed at a goddess, a dark chocolate lady and said, "You my Life is Like a

Box of Chocolates pretty. You never know what you're going to get." Again laughter filled the room. For the third chair I looked around to see who was ready to be chosen. I stopped on this quiet lady. I looked at her and saw her drop her head in shame as if she was not good enough to be chosen. I stopped right in front of her and said, "You, my sunshine, my sunshine. With a smile so bright that it would pierce its way through the blinds at sunrise to kiss me on the eyelids and wake me up in the worst mornings." She looked at me with question and surprise and mouthed, "Thank you." Just like that I filled up the hair wash stations. I made quick work with the towels and placed them around the collars of each of the ladies. As I turned on each of the faucets, I made sure to test the water temperature. "How is that?" I asked, "Is it warm enough?" They would respond with soft moans of affirmation. One by one I massaged their scalps in firm, gentle circles as I lathered then rinsed. Making sure not to let my fingers get tangled. One wash and rinse, and they were hooked. Everyone fell in love with me that day. I received hundreds of dollars in tips and enough hugs and kisses to have me smiling all week. From that day forward I had a new position. I was the official shampoo guy at the beauty salon. Ladies were requesting me, and my aunt wanted to know what I was doing to the women. "Everyone is requesting you, and only you to wash their hair," she said.

"It's a science Auntie."

She chuckled, "Okay nephew don't get in trouble over anything," and I said, "never that Auntie."

Before I knew it, graduation came and went. I planned to take a gap year. Before graduation my childhood friend David convinced me that we should be like Rambo and join the Army together in The Buddy Program. We were so hyped at the thought of shooting at enemies and running through the jungle, hacking away the hanging vines with our government issued machetes. We were excited and ready to do our part and become GI's. At the last minute I realized that the armed services just wasn't my thing and decided not to go. Even still, I had to admit that I was left empty and more than a little sad. David was going into the military, that meant no more weekend camping trips to the Chattahoochee River. It was the end of an era for us. High school was my social circle, and that too was over. Luckily, I continued to work in the salon and work on my charm, and it turned out to be an awesome summer.

Even though Atlanta was becoming a hub for the gay and lesbian community, homosexuality was not discussed in my small hometown. Our town was expanding, but everyone's minds were still closed. There was no talk of gays or any "alternative lifestyles". Gender roles were clearly defined. I worked at a hair salon, so I knew all about fashion and hair shows, which was something my friends had no interest in since it was a place where only women wanted to be, which was exactly where I wanted to be. For me it was a bachelor's paradise. My odds increased exponentially when I was with Jonathan.

Everyone loved Jonathan. He was tall, handsome, artistic, and a visionary. People from all over Atlanta came to have their hair "did" by him. Jonathan reveled in the celebrity status he had acquired. The only time his chair was empty was when he was not at the salon. He built a huge and loyal clientele and had been nominated as hairstylist of the year by the world renowned Bronner Brothers haircare products company. They sponsored and hosted the most popular hair show in the world that was happening in Atlanta this year. He was among the handful of men in hair design who would be showing off their skills at the 3 day event. Everyone was excited as it was an opportunity of a lifetime for him. He received vouchers for the most popular restaurants in Atlanta and accommodations at one of the finest hotels in Atlanta, Hotel Nikko, where he met three Puerto Rican sisters that had recently come from California. One of them had recently started working at the Nikko where he was staying for the hair show. Jonathan and Neida, the middle sister, clicked immediately. She was beautiful, single, had a strong, caring spirit. He was fascinated by her life and the places she'd lived in. He thought we would make the perfect couple. Jonathan was eager to play matchmaker, and being new in town, Neida was up to meeting the young handsome guy that her newfound friend kept going on and on about. As soon as the event was over for the night, he came back to the salon anxious to tell me about this lady.

"What does she look like?" I asked.

"She's bea-u-ti-ful," he answered, emphasizing every syllable as he pointed at me. "And very nice."

"What's her name?" I asked.

"It's either Rosa or Neida, one of those two."

He told me how much she made him laugh and how interesting she was. I circled back to her looks and her personality and once I was satisfied with his description of her I said, "Well, let me give it a shot." He gave me the number to the hotel, and I tried calling a couple of times. Not having her correct name posed a little bit of a challenge, especially since this was 1994 and calling Decatur was long-distance, so I couldn't call every day. I tried to call a couple of times and asked to speak with Nilda or Neida at the hotel, but whoever I spoke with said they weren't available or that they were either busy working or have not made it into work yet. Another time I was told there was no one by those names that worked there, so I just assumed her name was Nora. I still didn't know what she looked like. I had nothing to go on. No picture, no sketch, no in-person meeting, nothing! Jonathan had wanted us to meet at the salon one time, but that fell through. All I had to go on was his description and my imagination of how beautiful she was. I anticipated meeting this woman he was speaking so highly about. I even daydreamed about her.

All of a sudden, my life and schedule got very busy. Just like that, before I knew it 3 months had gone by. I went to the salon one day and Jonathan asked, "Have you had a chance to see or talk to the Puerto Rican princess yet?" I said, "No, not yet. I tried to call a few times but no luck in contacting her." He was so excited for us to meet. She must have put something in his spirit that we were meant to be. I made the decision I was going to get in my car that day and go and meet this lady that was meant for me, as Jonathan put it. After work I hit the road up to

Interstate 20 East heading to the Hotel Nikko. I was a little nervous and filled with anticipation at the thought of finally meeting her. I arrived at the hotel and parked. My heart felt like it was beating outside of my chest as I walked to the front lobby and right to the front desk.

"May I help you sir?" I looked at front desk agent with my huge smile and said, "Yes, is Rosa or Neida working today?" I said, "I think they work here?"

"Oh yes," she said with a soft voice. "Neida and Monti worked here. I knew them very well. They were the sweetest, funniest girls. They were from California." She kept going on about them and how fond she was of them. I listen intently and waited for a pause so I could politely interrupt. As soon as she paused I said, "You speak as if it's in the past." And she said, "Oh, I know. Yes, they left a couple of days ago heading back to California."

I said, "What! They're gone?"

She said, "Yes, they are. Did you know them?"

"Yes, oh, well. No. Not really." She looked confused. I said, "Someone that works for my aunt was actually trying to hook us up, and I heard that they work here too, at the hotel." I mentioned Jonathan, who of course she knew as well. I shrugged and said to her, "I guess if it was meant to be... it's mislaid love."

She chuckled, "I guess if you believe in that kind of stuff."

I dropped my head and thanked her for her time and headed back home.

The next day I went to the salon. As soon as I hit the door Jonathan came up beside me as if to tell me a secret and said, "I told you she was nice didn't I? Wasn't she beautiful? She is perfect!"

I looked at him in dead silence. When I didn't answer right away, he asked again. And I said, "Well brother, I wouldn't know."

He said, "What do you mean you wouldn't know?"

I said, "I wouldn't know because I never got a chance to see her."

"She was not there?" he asked.

"No, they're not there, they moved back to California a couple of days ago."

He said, "Man, I'm sorry. Well, maybe it just wasn't meant to be."

I said, "You know, as crazy it may seem, I don't feel that way. Maybe it's temporary and we might cross paths again."

He laughed out loud and said, "I guess you're going back to Cali? I don't think so!" He repeated the lyrics of a popular LL Cool J song.

So, I decided to choose to do something different. This missed opportunity really made me think. I felt like there was someone or something waiting for me somewhere. I needed to do something different.

I was a man of action, and I felt like I needed to do something to take my mind off of what I felt I had truly lost. I didn't know why I felt this way, but I felt like something special had just slipped from my grasp. I went home and signed up for the first SAT testing that was available. I studied a little and took the test, then waited for my score. I got a whole bunch of thoughts together in my head. What college did I want to attend? Should I stay in state and work? Go out of state and live on campus? So many decisions prompted by this one meeting that really never happened. If I had known her name maybe I would have been able to talk to her. Just Jonathan's description and my imagination of her beauty was not enough. Maybe Jonathan was right and we would have been great together. In my mind I pictured us holding hands and laughing at a private joke. Maybe we could have had a future. Thinking about her made me sadder knowing that I never even got the chance to meet her.

4

Los Angeles

Me and Judy had been working at an airport shuttle company when we got laid off. It was a blessing in disguise, had it not been for us being laid off from our jobs in Los Angeles, leaving California would have never been on our minds. As we packed our things in boxes and put our furniture in storage, we contemplated our move to Atlanta. We mapped out our route and picked a date. We called Mami and Papi, who by this time had been divorced for several years and let them know of our plans. Everyone was excited for us and our move to Atlanta and couldn't wait for our adventure to begin. Rosa was ready for a road trip. She was bored to death at home since her husband was in the Navy and had been deployed to Diego Garcia. She wanted to make the cross-country trip with us. The plan was for her to drive with us cross country, the three of us would be making our way from Los Angeles to Sacramento and then Atlanta and all points in between, then she would fly back when we were settled in. We were excited for our new adventure and road trip but sad to be leaving our family behind. I couldn't help but to think of how torn Mami and Papi had been when they left Puerto Rico so many years before. I was so sad, and I wished that everyone would just come with us. Mami reassured me that she would come visit soon, and Papi grabbed me squarely by the shoulders and said, "No tengas pena, cada quien tiene que buscar su por venir." He never held us back, just encouraged us to look for our own way of life. He had lived his life as he wanted and wanted us to do the same. He made sure that the car had fluids and told us to be careful. Off we went down the interstate highway.

Judy had just bought a brand new Ford Mustang, so we drove down through Nevada and Arizona without a care. It was summer and the temperature hovered just above 100 degrees, but we barely noticed as we drove with the air conditioner on full blast and our favorite CDs in the stereo. It wasn't until we had to gas up that we got out of the car and we felt the blazing heat. Every time we had to gas up, the suffocating heat made us rush back to the car. We had intended to visit some of the sites along the way but quickly abandoned that idea and decided to drive straight through as fast as we could. Destination: Atlanta, Georgia! We kept a good pace going through Texas, Louisiana, Mississippi, and Alabama, stopping only when we needed gas. It had already been three days and we were getting road weary, but once we saw the road sign welcoming us to

Georgia, we ignored the tiredness and filled with anticipation. We didn't mind the humidity in the air or the heat. We got into Atlanta in the early evening and called our friend Kevin to let him know we had made it in and started looking for a motel where we could stay for as long as it took us to find an apartment. We had come prepared and knew where we wanted to look for a place. The coordinators at the unemployment office in Los Angeles gave us a couple of tips and helped us map out the city which was abuzz with activity and teaming with possibilities. The Olympics would be hosted by Atlanta in two years, and it seemed like the anticipation had everyone in a great mood. We met with our friend Kevin. We'd known him since we lived in Sacramento. He and his two best friends had a rap group and whenever we were in the same city, we were inseparable. He'd been in Atlanta for 2 years and he knew where the hot spots were, and he wanted to show us his adopted town. It seemed like no matter where we went in Atlanta everything was "Peachtree this" and "Peachtree that!" We got lost more than a couple of times looking for Peachtree Street when we should have been looking for Peachtree Way. Kevin showed us downtown and the business district, Midtown, CNN, the Coca-Cola museum, College Park, and of course the birthplace of Martin Luther King Jr. I noticed that the highways were not as crowded as the LA freeways, but it was congested nonetheless. On the streets there was foot traffic galore. There were young people everywhere. I asked Kevin why it was so busy? He said, "Girl, you in the middle of Freaknik and the hair show!" The girls and

I looked at each other and then at Kevin and paused because we had no idea what either one of those things were.

We went to a motel and inquired about vacancies and were lucky enough to find a spot that was reasonably priced. We checked in, unpacked our stuff, and even though it was getting late, went outside to join the street party. It seemed like everyone had come to Atlanta. We met people who like us had come to Atlanta for the job opportunities. Others, the younger ones, were here strictly here for the fun of Freaknik or the allure of the hair show. Everywhere you looked there were throngs of young people in one activity or another. At the city parks, the school campuses, the city center. The music was loud, and the vibe was energetic, electric and contagious. The best way I could describe Freaknik was a huge family picnic, it was MTV's Spring Break on steroids.

The next day we had to find a realtor to help us find an apartment and line up some prospects for jobs. These things were very time-consuming because it was in an era way before smartphones and the internet, so we had to use the Yellow Pages and Thomas Brothers Guide Maps. The highways were confusing for us as well as the streets. Luckily, Atlanta was full of southern hospitality. There was not a shortage of people willing to help us. Everyone's first question to us was always, "Are you a Georgia Peach?" You couldn't help but to be amused by the question and the accent. For me being in Georgia was not that different than being in California except that instead of seeing brown faces we saw plenty of beautiful Black Faces. The unemployment office was the same. It wasn't too crowded, and our counselor was very helpful in providing us leads for jobs. There were plenty of opportunities everywhere, not just in Atlanta. I'd been a receptionist at Prime Time Shuttle in Los Angeles, so naturally I was looking for a job doing something similar. I didn't think that it would be hard to acquire a job in any of the hotels or offices that were popping up everywhere. A couple of days after we arrived in Atlanta, we met with a realtor who took us around DeKalb and Decatur showing us apartment after apartment. We only knew that we wanted an apartment in a nice area close to the expressway, reasonably priced, and with plenty of amenities. And that's what we got. It didn't take us very long to find one. We moved out of the motel, moved into the apartment, and started looking for jobs more aggressively. I found a job at the Sheraton Hotel, which was literally across the street from the apartments. But because the expressway was only a one way I had to jump on the expressway and then circle back. With a job and an apartment, a great burden was lifted, and I felt I could relax. Southern hospitality made it easy to make friends at work and on the street. When people heard me speak, they asked if I was from the north. I'd be at a loss because although I was raised in Boston, I had just recently come from California, and obviously I couldn't hear my own accent. I didn't know how I should answer. And what did they be mean by Northern? I had no clue so most times I just laughed it off. I'd been hired as a PBX operator in the back office of the Sheraton which was easy enough. While training at the front desk we helped a guy named Jonathan. We struck up a conversation and quickly became friends. He'd come over during the day and tell us about the hair salon where he worked. We learned that hair was to Atlanta what entertainment was to Los Angeles. Rosa had a head full of long, black hair, and he kept asking her to be his model for the hair show. We had no idea how big the hair culture was here! Here hair was both art and the medium. The only thing we knew about hair was that no matter how much Aqua Net white can we would use, it was no match for the down-home relative humidity. Most nights we'd leave the apartment with bouncy curls only to have a bushy helmet of hair as soon as we got out of the car. Our only recourse was to wear it slicked back or braided which didn't feel very attractive to us and much too subdued compared to the hair styles we saw around town. We thought asymmetrical hairstyles were daring, but here we saw sky high up-do's, floor-length tresses, and hairstyles accessorized with everything from chains and shells, to bird cages and fishbowls. It was amazing!

The salon that Jonathan worked at on the weekends was owned by Miss Sandra, it was always busy he said. With the hair show and Freaknik it was a madhouse. He had planned on taking us around to see more of Atlanta over the weekend, but the morning had gotten away from him and now he was swamped. He offered to have Miss Sandra's nephew go with us in his place, but he was coming from Newnan and he said it would be about an hour or so before he'd be able to meet with us. We didn't want to wait around at the salon and be under foot, so we decided we'd see the "real" Atlanta another day and headed to the Jimmy Carter Presidential Library instead. Thankfully we only got lost once and were able to get our bearings pretty quickly. We found the library and were surprised to learn that this was not the type of library where you could borrow books. It was more of a museum rather than a library. I can only imagine what the docents were thinking when we asked, "Where are the books that we can read through and check out?" They must have thought we were a special kind of stupid. We laughed it off and headed for lunch at Varsity. Everyone told us it was the best spot for a great burger, and it didn't disappoint. We made it there without getting lost and we hung out for a while there with everyone else, although we hadn't intended to. It was packed with people trying to get a bite to eat and a date. Atlanta was turning out to be a great spot for us and just as we were getting comfortable, we got a call from Hiram in California. Papi had fallen and hurt his foot and due to his diabetes had to have part of his foot amputated. It was very serious, and he was in the hospital for several days. We were in shock. Papi had never been seriously ill and the thought of him being alone in the hospital was too much for us to bear. What if he didn't make it? Who would take care of him? We decided the only thing we could do was drive back to California and make sure we were there to take care of him.

By this time, I was working at both the Sheraton and at the Hotel Nikko. I put in my notice and let them know I was going back to California to see about Papi. We called our realtor and let her know that we'd be leaving, and we were westbound in less than two weeks out. We'd only

been in Atlanta for about six months, but we knew with
our stay being cut so short that we would greatly miss it.

$\sim$

Back in Sacramento, California

Our trip back to California was a lot more somber than
we wanted to admit. It was just me and Judy since Rosa
had flown back already. All I could think of was how en-
thusiastic Papi was when we told them we were leaving.
He was sad but never wanted to hold us back. When we
called to tell him that we had an apartment and that we'd
made friends and had jobs he was so happy for us. We
knew that he had diabetes, he had it since we were in Boston, but we thought it was under control. I had never seen
Papi sick and took all of my strength not to cry all the way
back to California. Georgia would always be here, but Papi
was my dad and I couldn't imagine not having him in my
life at least not yet. Arriving back in California was not
bittersweet, it was exciting. I was happy that I was back
and able to see Papi again. We went to see him at the
hospital, and as soon as we got in I got a chance to speak
with his doctor who was very optimistic. He only had to
amputate his baby toe and part of his foot because he got
an infection and couldn't feel it because of his neuropathy.
The worst part was that he'd recently become septic and
needed infusion therapy. We thought we'd be taking him
home, but instead he was being transferred to a different
facility for 30 days while they administered his antibiotics.

I had no idea that people died from sepsis! I felt so helpless and uninformed. That night I decided that I would learn as much as I could about whatever was going on with Papi and take care of him. While he was at the facility, I got everything ready for when he came home. His doctor was very conservative and made sure they only amputated the barest minimum, but he excavated in such a way that he left a gaping hole that had to be packed twice daily.

I met with his nurse Janice and learned how to change and pack his wounds, and I learned how and when to give him his medication. I was happy and willing to do it. The hardest part was reminding Papi of how seriously sick he was. He wanted to get up and do whatever he normally did because he couldn't feel a lot of the pain coming from the wound. He was compliant, and although he was accustomed to being out and about for as long as he had been by himself, he was an easy patient. As long as he had his cordless phone and remote control within reach of his Lazy Boy he was fine.

In the mornings after breakfast and after his medications I'd remove his bandages and soak his feet. Somehow this became a beautiful bonding time between us. We talked about his life, his family back in Puerto Rico, and Mami. Being the oldest son, he always made sure that his brothers and sisters were taken care of. They had the utmost respect for Papi, even as adults it was "yes sir", or "no sir". When he talked about Mami he'd always talk about the mistakes he'd made with her. He confessed that he never dreamed they would ever separate. Astonished and bewildered, I thought to myself, really?! Not even during your alcohol-fueled tirades? Or the weekly impromptu boxing matches? I could see the pain in his eyes, but still I wondered if time had blurred his memory or if he really thought that after all of what she went through she would still stay with him. I never asked him, but I did ask Mami many years later to see what her recollection was.

5

Boston, Massachusetts

I don't remember what happened, but it seemed like all of a sudden Papi was coming home from work drunk and angry. I can't say that he abused us because it didn't feel like that. He used to come home drunk, slam all the doors, and knock over every chair and sofa that was in his way whether it had someone in it or not. He would demand something to eat but then yell if it wasn't what he wanted. My poor Mami never argued but tried to appease him until he took it too far and swung on her. She would push all of us kids out of the room and try to reason with Papi. He never listened. We all knew what was coming next, it was going to be a brawl. That's why I think I never viewed it as abuse because Mami never cowered away, she never ran to her room, and never let Papi get the best of her. All of us slowly made our way to the living room where the *action was unfolding, and we sat atop the sofa that was still toppled over, and we started to cheer my mom on. Papi would swing and miss, but Mami would punch with all her might and land every time. He'd grab her hair, and she'd kick him in the gut, solid. He'd come at her almost in slow motion, but she'd evade him until he finally threw the last punch and landed on the floor. "Mami wins again!" is all we could say as we all went to Papi and sat around him. My parents separated when I was five. I remember leaving in the middle of the night while Papi slept off another night of drinking. Hiram and Angel were old enough to help carry trash bags full of our clothes that Mami had kept by the door for this exact occasion. For the last couple of weeks, Mami had been washing and sorting our clothes. She'd set aside two large trash bags. One was filled with clothes to keep and one with old and badly worn clothes to throw away. As luck would have it, Hiram and Angel took the bags intended to be thrown away, but we only realized it once we got to my aunt's house which was about 16 city blocks away. Mami didn't know how to drive so we walked.*

I wasn't scared. I wasn't sad. I suppose I was too young to understand what was happening. Once we got to my aunt's house there was a whirlwind of silent activity since my uncle was asleep and so were my cousins. We were ushered into a room, girls in with the girls. Boys in with the boys. Mami ended up with the girls at the foot of our bed. The following morning, we woke up and all went to school like it was any other regular day. As an adult I often wondered how my father reacted the moment when he woke up and found himself alone with no wife, no children, and no family. I know that I would have been devastated. If Mami knew anything about Papi she knew he wouldn't let us go without a fight. We'd been at my aunt's house for a couple of weeks, and aside from being a little crowded I didn't notice too much of a difference. Then one afternoon when we were playing outside, I was sitting on the ground playing with sidewalk chalk and my cousins and sister were playing in front of me. Out of nowhere I heard them all yelling my name. It was like everything was moving in slow motion and in silence. I couldn't understand them because they were all yelling at the same time. I looked at Rosa and tried to pay attention only to her scared voice as she screamed, "Papi is coming to grab you!" I looked back just in time to see my father two steps away from me, arms outstretched and ready to grab me. I was scared because from my spot on the ground he looked so big and so angry. My heart was pounding. Instinctively I got up to where my sister was jumping with her outstretched hands. I reached her and she grabbed me, and we ran back to the house.

Mami was so shaken. She didn't believe that Papi would actually come try and snatch us. She decided then and there that we'd have to move out of Boston. My mother called up a friend who agreed to let us stay with her for a couple of days, so the next morning my uncle drove us the hour and a half and we were on our way to Springfield. When we got there Mami's friend reconsidered, so we had to find somewhere else to go. Mami called other friends she knew, but there were just too many of us. She finally called the women's shelter in the area that said they take us, but Hiram couldn't come because at 12 he was just too old. I heard the anger and disbelief when they tried to explain to my mother that her twelve-year-old was practically a threat to the other clients at the shelter. A friend of a friend felt sorry for us and let us spend two nights at his house. Mami didn't speak much English, but she was very resourceful and on the third day we packed up and moved to our semi-furnished apartment in Holyoke, Massachusetts. It was a 5-story building, and we spent a lot of time by ourselves after school because Mami had a job in one of the factories and Hiram was supposed to watch us. But all we did was eat ketchup and mayonnaise sandwiches after school and play Batman and Robin on the porch out back. Looking back now I can't believe how carefully we were swinging off of the fifth-floor railings like we were on solid ground. We could have fallen and been seriously hurt. Lucky for us we didn't spend too much time in Holyoke, though Papi found out where we were and demanded to see us. After a lot of yelling and debating Mami conceded and called us out to the front stairs because Papi wasn't allowed in the house. As soon as he was gone she took us all upstairs and got on the phone to call around to find out who had told Papi where we were. After she called all her friends and family and practically everyone she knew, we found out that her younger sister Annie, who she hadn't talked to since we left Boston, had told Papi where we were. Mami confronted her and yelled, "Porque Le dijiste?" My aunt said Papi was so sad and practically crying asking about us. That she

couldn't bear him coming around day after day and pleading with her to tell him. Mami and Papi argued daily until
Papi told her he didn't care about her or what she did. He
just cared about his kids, and if she wanted to keep moving, he'd keep looking because she'd never be able to keep
him away from his kids. We moved back to Boston because
Mami had no other choice. We stayed with my aunt for
almost a year even though Annie had four children and
Mami had five. We were cramped tight until Mami got us
our own place. I guess it was payment for snitching on us.

Papi was happy because he knew exactly where we were,
and Mami was happy because we didn't have to leave
again. Mami finally got us into our own apartment, not
too far from where we were, which meant that we were
able to finally settle into a little bit of routine and a little
bit of normalcy. After that we moved from Jamaica Plain
to Dorchester. Papi was never allowed inside our house.
He'd honk his horn and we'd run out and visit with him
in his car. Some days we would just sit and talk, and he'd
ask about our days. In other times he took us out to eat at
McDonald's which to us was like being taken to the Ritz.
As required by Mami, Papi gave us a weekly allowance
from $2 to $5, and on our birthdays he'd give us $15 to
spend it on whatever we wanted. As Hiram, Angel, and
Rosa got older, they found better things to do than sit in
the car with Papi for his weekly visits, so it ended up being Judy and me. I loved it because I had him practically
to myself and with just the two of us, we did more. He'd
take us on long rides, he took us to the grocery store to

buy our favorite breakfast cereal, and in the summer he took us to the lake to buy a soda pop and cotton candy.

I looked forward to Papi's visits and loved how interested he was in my life. He took an interest that Mami didn't. He did ask me about school, he'd ask me about my hobbies, and one particular summer he helped me plant a vegetable garden. Papi knew and understood me, and we liked each other. If I ever came home from school and saw Papi's car double parked out front of our house, I knew it must be bad. Hiram, Angel, and Rosa we're always getting into some kind of trouble. Smoking, shoplifting, cutting class, and when Mami worked nights it was wild, late night parties. He'd come in for the discipline emergencies, and Mami would give him a rundown of the situation. Without saying a word, he would take off his belt, give each of them their punishment, and leave as quietly as he'd come. Papi didn't live with us anymore, but he was always present in our lives. We moved from Dorchester to Puerto Rico, and he made sure to call us frequently and send money for us regularly. When we moved from Puerto Rico to California, Papi followed just six months later.

All these years later we still liked each other. I would do anything for him, and he would do anything for me. I would not think twice about taking care of him for as long as he needed me. We shared a lot as I soaked his feet and change his bandages. Mami moved us around because of him, yet there was never a time that I was without him. He made us his priority. I don't think that made him special, that made him my father.

Mami said it was harder for her to stay than it was to leave. In 1960, she thought the world was going to end before she even got a chance to have children. She didn't want to die before she'd gotten married and had the full experience. Papi was just a means to an end. I knew she didn't love him anymore, but to know that she never loved him was a surprise. I thought that there might have been some semblance of love for her to have five children with him. In my mind he had swept her off her feet and played her love songs on his cuatro. I thought he'd written her love notes to tell her how much he loved her. They had none of that. To hear Mami tell it, theirs was nothing more than a business arrangement, except Papi wasn't in on the arrangement. Knowing that made me feel very sad for him because he had no idea that he never had a fighting chance. I was very protective of Papi. Even when I was younger everyone including Mami knew not to bad-mouth Papi in front of me. Mami was still young and like every other Cosmopolitan woman liked to look good. She always had her hair done nicely and her makeup was flawless. There was never a shortage of admirers. Whenever she got together with her friends the conversation would inevitably come to her and Papi's separation. If I was in the room my eyes would shoot daggers at anyone no matter who if they ever dare to say the wrong thing about him. If they ignored my daggers, I'd get vocal and point out to whoever it was that they didn't know my father and therefore had no permission to speak about him. Most of the time they would ask how he could leave such a beauty like Mami or how lovesick he must be

now that they were apart, but I didn't want to hear any
of it. I knew it wasn't my place, but I didn't care. Mami
made sure that I wasn't in earshot when her friends came
over and if I walked in, she quickly changed the subject. I
knew that she begrudgingly conceded that small victory to
me and in return I stayed out of her way. I knew that Hiram, Angel, and Rosa were occupying most of her time with
all their friends, teenage angst, and troubles. I made sure I
never got bad grades or hung around the wrong crowds. She
was free to concentrate her time on her job, her dates, and
the other kids, and I felt like I practically parented myself.

$$\backsim$$

California

Papi healed nicely and life got back to normal for us.
I got a job offer in Los Angeles, so I moved back to Los
Angeles from Sacramento. And although I'd enjoyed life
in Los Angeles for over 13 years, I found that it had become drab. I was in a big city full of people, but I was
by myself even though I had plenty of friends. I longed for
the lasting and meaningful relationships that I remember
my parents having when I was young. Friends that would
come over and visit for hours. Friends that shared what
they had without keeping tabs or expecting anything in return. Friends that saw you in need and stepped in to help
without being asked. I wasn't sure if what I was looking for
didn't exist anymore, or if I was just in the wrong place. I
knew it wouldn't be easy, but I was ready for a change. A

change of pace, a change of scenery and a change of life. Growing up my family always moved around from place to place. A lot of times not in the best circumstances. We had moved from Puerto Rico to New York, then Massachusetts, and back to Puerto Rico, California, Georgia and back to California. Every time a difference experience, and a chance to grow and learn new things about the world, my parents, and myself. I learned to have an adventurous spirit and a unique view of the world.

I had made a list of places I wanted to live and narrowed it down to three places. Florida, Virginia, and Texas. Florida because I was excited for the kind of community I would be a part of there, in Los Angeles Puerto Ricans were few and far between. I wanted to be around people who spoke like me and had things in common with me. I was sure I'd find kinship there. Florida was full of Puerto Ricans! Virginia because I'd be close enough to the East coast but not exactly in it and I'd get to experience the change of seasons again, although not as harsh as Boston. Texas made the list because I'd always wanted to visit the South and looking at the map Virginia didn't seem that Southern to me. In Texas I figured I'd get to experience the South while still being in a metropolitan area. I gave myself a year to do some research, save some money, and give notice at my job. Basically, get my ducks all in a row so I could mitigate any unforeseen circumstances. Spring in Los Angeles brought on the countdown to my big move. I was excited.

6

Arkansas
Big Move

Rosa had been divorced and had recently moved to Arkansas for a fresh start. She invited me to visit her for Easter break. While there I talked to her about my desire to move out of Los Angeles and about the cities I was considering and she asked, "Why don't you think about moving to Arkansas?" I gave her a crazy look and puzzled I responded, "Pffft, why would I want to live in Arkansas?" I didn't even know why SHE had decided to move to Arkansas! And just as I said it, I thought to myself...I'm alone in Los Angeles and I'd be alone in Florida, Virginia, or Texas. While it was true that Arkansas was never even on my list, I liked what I saw. Arkansas was a small southern state, and Little Rock was a thriving metropolitan area with great potential. "Why NOT Arkansas?" I thought, and just like that Arkansas became my destination.

I took advantage of my visit to look at the city objectively. To Rosa's credit, she didn't go for the hard sell. Instead as we went around town, we talked about how it reminded us of Puerto Rico with the humidity and the smell of moisture in the air. Arkansas was called the Natural State for good reason, there was lush greenery everywhere you looked. The more I looked, the more ready I was to leave the big city behind and be somewhere that wasn't so crowded, so fast paced, and so noisy. Somewhere I could rise to the sounds of nature, of birds chirping and fall asleep to the calming sounds of crickets. I was happy with my new choice and Rosa reasoned if I ended up not liking it, I would be close to my original choices and could just move on. I gave myself a year. I figured that would be enough time to consider my options if I wanted to and tie up any loose ends.

Los Angeles, California

My farewell year came and went so fast! I decided I wanted to see as much as I could of California before I actually said farewell, so I went down the California coast and visited Mami in Sacramento. I drove over the Golden Gate Bridge, which by the way, is not golden. I traveled through California's Central Valley stopping at as many fruit stands as I could all the way down the interstate back to Los Angeles, Southern California to take in the sights that I'd been too busy to visit in the 13 years that I had lived there. Chinatown, Koreatown, Filipinotown. The Garment District, the Flower District, and just for kicks, the Diamond District. Hollywood and Vine, the Hollywood sign and Hollywood Studios. Venice Beach, Zuma Beach, and Topanga Beach. Museum of Tolerance, Museum of Contemporary Art, and the J Paul Getty Museum. So many places that I didn't realize that I hadn't seen. I knew I would never get to everything that everyone came to California to see but just making a list was fun. Just as fun as visiting all the restaurants I knew I'd never eat at again and miss so much.

The time came and I tearfully said goodbye to my friends, gave notice at work, and turned in my apartment keys. With boxes packed and my route to Arkansas mapped out, I embarked on a journey that would prove to be life changing. I didn't want to be overly dramatic, but I was more than cautiously optimistic. I had a good feeling. I was in total control of this trip. I was giddy with excitement. I had planned on making the drive to Arkansas by myself, but Rosa had surprised me and volunteered to drive with me.

"You know I never say no to a good road trip!"

"I know girl, here we go again."

This would be our 2nd cross-county trip. We had made a similar trip so many years before when the three of us, me, her and Judy, had decided to drive to Georgia. This time we wouldn't rush, to combat the tedium Rosa had looked online and had noted points of interest along the way. Gassed up and buckled in, we were off on mile number one of one thousand six hundred and sixty eight.

As we drove down the 10 Interstate, I found myself feeling a little melancholy. I was excited for my new adventure.

I'd planned for a year and was leaving Los Angeles with no regrets, but I was sad that this part of my life was over, sad that I'd be leaving friends that I was really going to miss. I couldn't help but think back to all the times that Mami had to make her moves with all of us kids in tow. I imagined how sad she must have been, and I realized just then how hard it must have been for her to have to keep moving all those times, not just escaping her abusive marriage, but also looking for a better life for us. I cried for Mami because I understood.

We made it a point to drive as much as we could during the hot days and stop for the night when we couldn't keep our eyes open anymore. Which worked out great because driving in the day you could clearly see the changing land-scape. The sage brush and Joshua trees of California gave way to the giant Saguaro cactus of Arizona. They looked so comical sprouting up in the distance like green men holding up their arms in surrender. While in Arizona we stopped in Lake Havasu to get a look at the real London Bridge. It was really unassembled in London, England and reas-sembled brick by brick in Lake Havasu, Arizona-America! What an engineering marvel. We passed the Painted Desert and reached the Grand Canyon in the middle of the night, we didn't stop. I'm sure it would have been a fantastic site in the light of day, but at night it was just dark and scary. There was no way we were brave enough to wait with the coyotes and the rattlers until morning. Viewing the Grand Canyon would have to be an adventure for another day. We made quick work of New Mexico and the pink des-ert mountains. Rosa looked up from her phone and said,

"...Hey, let's stop at the Cadillac Ranch and see what that's about."

"Sure, I'm up for a little detour, let's go to the ranch!"

I made sure we had enough gas and we made our way there. It wasn't too out of the way and luckily it was daytime. We pulled up to see a whole bunch of cars, I guess Cadillacs half buried in the ground. You are welcome to take a stab at graffiti art with spray paint and leave your mark on the cars and we did. It was a fun distraction and after we took some pictures for posterity and social media we were back on our way. Thankfully we had emptied our bladders, got snacks, and gassed up because by this time I was tired of Texas and ready to be in Arkansas. We kept a good pace and got to Oklahoma and saw some buffalo on the side of the road next to a souvenir store. It made me a little sad to think that here it was all alone when it used to roam the whole land.

7
Welcome to Arkansas

*I*t was a relief to finally be driving into Arkansas. It was just as it was last year. The air was moist and smelled of burning wood, the trees were green, and it reminded me of the drives through Canton that Papi used to take us when were little.

Rosa was a gracious host. She said, "Stay as long as you need to." I was grateful because although I had started looking for a job in Arkansas while I was still in Los Angeles, it's still good not to have that burden of needing a place to stay. The weather in Little Rock was beautiful, so on weekends I'd help Rosa with her vegetable garden which was her new project. I already knew how labor-intensive a garden was because Papi had helped me plant one in Boston. We headed to our nearest home improvement store to start on our garden. As I looked through the rack of seed packets, I realized we were too late for seeds. According to the back of the packets for our zones we should *have started two months ago! Undeterred from our mission, we bought some seedlings. It wasn't cheating because everyone was doing it by the looks of it. We got seedlings for everything we wanted in a salad. Butter lettuce, red lettuce, tomatoes, onions, bell peppers, sweet basil, cilantro and cucumbers. We had to buy gloves, hats, shovels, and bags of planting mix, and we had to get tools to hoe, tools to turn over the dirt, and tools to carry the dirt. Once we got back to our garden, we had to lay down planting fabric, then we had to form little mounds in rows of the dirt where we would put our plants. It seemed a little excessive for a salad, but we were excited and ready for some hard work. The rows were planted and looking fresh and earthy. Dirty and exhausted, we sat down on some used wooden pallets (that would be another project) and had some cold sweet tea, which I just recently found out was a southern staple. We sat and sipped and watched the sky darken and pour down rain. What?!? We had just planted AND watered the plants, and it looked like now all the rain in the sky would drown them. We quickly got up, rushed inside, and got some plastic bags and as the rain continued to fall, we secured each little plant with its own personalized makeshift greenhouse. Proud of our industrious work and quick-thinking, we went back over to the pallets and sat back down to our sweet tea and relaxed to the sounds of the rain.*

I've always loved the sound of the rain. In Puerto Rico we could see the rain coming over the hillsides, and if we had laundry on the clothesline drying Mami would yell from upstairs, "Ahi viene la lluvia, corran y agarren la ropa ante' que se moje!" (Hey you guys the rain is coming, let's hurry and take the clothes off of the line before it gets wet with rain.) We would deliberately stand outside and let the rain come down on us while Mami stood in the front door telling us to hurry up and come inside before the lightning started. To me it seemed like rain always had his own personality. In Boston, the rain was deliberate. It would come down as predicted and in straight sheets to clean the streets, to clean your cars, and wash away the trash and dirt. I'd watch as the dirty water made its way down the gutter and into the sewers. In Puerto Rico, the rain came down unexpected and many times during the day. Often times it was gentle as it washed away debris. It bought new life, and it swelled up the rivers and filled up our water containers. In California, just like the song said, it hardly ever rained. There were times when I'd buy an umbrella and galoshes and never use them. When it would finally come down it would be hard, dark, cold rain where it would create mudslides and flood out apartment complex parking lots. Everyone would comment how bad it was but then in the same sentence how much we really needed it. In Arkansas, the weather would change from one moment to the next. It could be sunny in the morning and in the afternoon there'd be a downpour and in the evening sun again and a little breezy. I figured out that if I wanted to outsmart the weather, I'd better carry an umbrella everywhere I went. I carried an umbrella in my purse and in the car, in my desk at work, and another in my apartment. But now I was learning that the rain could be a little more than an inconvenience. I was relieved to learn that I had missed a couple of deadly tornadoes that happened a month before I got to Arkansas. The meteorologist would predict precipitation, which meant you got what you got. Rain, drizzle, hail, sleet, snow...that's right, snow! The hail would damage your car, the sleet would ruin your drive in from work. The rain would flood the street, and the snow would stop the city dead in its tracks. Rosa's poor little garden that we had just diligently planted three days ago was now a casualty of the unpredictable Arkansas weather. She called me. "Oh my gosh!" she said, "The wind and rain took up all the little plants!" and when I went by her house to look at the disaster the only thing remaining were the fabric sheets that were once under all the dirt and plants. All I could think of was, "Man, that was one expensive salad."

8

North Carolina

My first day as a college freshman was a breeze. To me it felt like high school except we lived at school and my social game was on point. You would guess that being from a small town I'd be homesick and feel awkward, but no, I was in my element. I loved meeting knew people and learning as much as I could about them. Every person I met was a new friend. I realized that no matter where you are, people are inherently nice and helpful. I purposely left my books in my dorm when I went to class. It gave me a reason to ask a classmate, usually a girl, if I could read along with her. If I needed to take notes I'd ask for a sheet of paper. Always banking on my Southern charm I'd never lose. My parents and grandparents had invested solidly in my future education, so I didn't have finances to worry about. I was free to think about other things in my college life like partying and the ladies. I wanted to expand my social circle outside of campus so when I heard some students talking about an available 3rd shift clerk position at a local gas station, I jumped at the chance. It was perfect for me; I'd never needed much sleep, and I could study during the slow times. The next day I went to the interview and poured on the charm. Naturally, they fell in love with me and I began my work journey.

While working at my day job I had a couple of big heads in upper level management take interest and appreciation of my work ethics. This one guy in particular, Paul Ross, took a liking to me. They came to me and offered a position in North Carolina! Deep down in my soul I was yearning an opportunity like this, a change much needed in my life at the time. I wanted to leave and didn't want to be stuck in Whitesburg, which seemed to be dead end for me. I kept calm and thanked everyone for their consideration. They told me to take the weekend and go to the West Industries in Franklin, North Carolina. I woke up early Saturday morning and headed out to check out my new city and begin one of the most memorable chapters in my life. While arriving to the location, I couldn't believe it. I had been to this part of the country before. Seeing all the beautiful mountains triggered an extreme case of nostalgia. I had wanted to come back to this area for so long. It was all coming back to me. My family took a vacation to Maggie Valley the Ghost town in the sky when I was 15. I remembered riding in the back seat of Daddy's Oldsmobile Cutlass Salon Coupe staring out the window thinking that I would love to live here one day, and now I was a "YES" away from accepting the position and allowing my dreams of a child to come true. I toured the facility where I would be working and met some of the staff. I knew after that this place was going be it, so I decided to look around for places to live. I immediately got some suggestions from the coworkers at the job. I headed to the first place. The property manager Carol was not from North Carolina originally, she explained to me that her husband had been injured while working for the railroad and had received a settlement, which they invested in the rental properties. Carol was a beautiful lady. Her husband never fully recovered from the accident and stayed in bed the majority of the time. I fell in love with the place and signed the lease immediately.

While coming back home from school one evening, Ms. Carol met me at the mailbox and asked "Marcel, could you come visit with us after you get settled?"

"Sure," I said, wondering what in the world would they need to see me about. I did a quick inventory in my mind of anything that I might have done. I'd only been a tenant for about 6 months, and I'd never been late with my rent. I was never loud enough to cause a ruckus. I pretty much stayed to myself, so I doubted anyone would complain about me. I showered and headed over to their unit. I gently knocked on the door. "Ms. Carol...?" I said just in a little over a whisper in hopes she wouldn't hear me. I knocked again, still no answer. As I turned to walk away the door flew open.

"Hi Marcel, come in we have been expecting you!" She stepped to the side and let me in. "What can I get you to drink?"

Not wanting to be rude I said I would take some ice water with extra ice. She bought the ice water and asked me to follow her to the bedroom. My mind was racing. Was I getting evicted? Did she want to sleep with me? I really didn't want to mess up my living situation by sleeping with the owner's wife! I slowly walked down the hall, glancing in every room till I came close to the bedroom. She yelled out, "Back here Marcel." I peeked in and heard his voice, "Marcel, welcome! How are you?" Before I could think I said, "I am wonderful sir, and yourself?"

It was her husband laid up in bed like a patient in a hospital with the sheets tucked tightly at his sides. I asked, "How is everything with you!" He chuckled. "Well, I have been better...Well Marcel, I'm sure your wondering why we invited you here," he said. I was hoping he wasn't thinking what I was thinking because I was convinced he was calling me over to join his private swinging community.

"Yes, just a little," I said as I took a sip of water.

"As you can see my situation I can't really help with the upkeep of the place. We were hoping you could help Carol a little bit and be our facilities manager. Of course we would compensate you and reduce your rent accordingly." I exhaled loudly in relief and jumped at the chance. "Yes, of course! No problem. I'd love to help out." I did plenty of maintenance work around my own house and with my Granddaddy. It was a breeze. It also helped that the property was already immaculate. Ms. Carol was very sweet, and she'd call me over for simple stuff. I'm sure she just needed someone to talk to. I was happy to oblige. I was by myself and learning how people outside of my small town lived. For the first time in my life, I was defining who I was. I found out who I was, maybe because I was the only person of color or because of my youth, but it helped me realize that people liked me and gravitated towards me.

I had finished my freshman year with a bang, and I was beginning the New Year with renewed confidence. During Christmas break I went home, and my grandfather informed me that he was sick and needed help getting to his doctor visits. He was stoic and matter of fact when he asked me to help him. I saw the fear in his eyes, and I flashed back to the tall, strong man who carried me on his shoulders. I saw him looking defeated and unsure. The thought of losing him never crossed my mind. For him to tell me he was dying felt like the rug was being pulled out from under me. All my life my granddaddy was the person I looked up to, he was the one that instilled a sense of pride in me. I saw him go to work every day, and the way he loved his family was obvious in everything he did. My grandmother was elderly as well and more than inconvenience or burden her, he didn't want to scare her. Even in his sickness he was taking care of others. The smart and caring man who read the newspaper out loud while I sat on his lap was dying. For the first time ever, I was afraid for him. I made my decision right then. I owed him. He had been there for me my entire life. I had a debt to pay, my heart was heavy, but I was ready to pay up. Without a second thought I packed up my stuff and moved back to Whitesburg to see about my Granddaddy.

I came back home, and I was able to see how his illness had taken a toll on him in such a short time. My poor Granddaddy had such a hard time breathing he had to sleep sitting up. His once firm grip was shaky and unsteady. He had ALS and even though he was sick I was confident that he would get better, and I would do all I could to make sure of it. Our days consisted of doctor visits, diagnostic testing, and treatment, and more doctor visits. After one particularly exhausting day of appointments, Granddaddy could barely walk. I saw him struggling, so I ran over to help him and had him lean on me as I eased him into his chair. I would have carried him like that for the rest of his life if I had to. Granddaddy had worked hard and took care of his family, yet his son, my father, didn't come to his aid but reprimanded him for his weakness. I was so angered at what I felt was an utterly inappropriate reaction to my Granddaddy's ill health. All I wanted to do was punch my father right in the face. I took care of Granddaddy for 2 years when a cardiac arrest finally took his life.

I started a new job in Atlanta and a new chapter in my life. Prior to that, I had an e-commerce pet business that I had successfully grown, and I was able to sell it for a great profit. I lived off of those profits for two years. One day I looked into my bank account and realized that I had to return to the working class as my money had run out, so I was back in the rat race. I had a home boy named Tyrone who had reached out to me about a job opportunity with a building supply company that was much like the company we had worked together in the past. He thought I might do well in one of the operations positions that was just vacated. He talked it up real good. I put on my Sunday best and went to the interview on a Friday, and I started working the following Monday.

Being back in the working word was definitely a bit of a struggle in the beginning. The mornings were cold and there were days when I had to be on top of an exposed building with no walls to block the cold wind along with the cold temperatures. Several guys that started with me didn't make the cut. They couldn't make it through the morning much less the afternoon. At that very moment I thought of something Granddaddy said to me years ago when he was working with Georgia Power in the late 50s. He was dealing with a lot of discrimination as a lot of them were, and he had to undergo a lot of humiliation and degradation. It started out he said with a bunch of guys who weren't always treated fairly or as well as they should have. Several of the guys couldn't tolerate any more aggression, racism, and violence, so they quit in frustration. My grandfather told me, "I had to take care of my family. I had people who depended on me, so I tolerated it with prayer and the belief that it would get better." He stayed at Georgia Power for 40 years and moved up as much as his education would allow. He only went to the 8th grade. Knowing this, I persevered at my job going from construction site to construction site with my Granddaddy on my mind, guiding me the whole time.

I had kept in contact with many of my friends from high school and David especially. Throughout the years we had shared our experiences and lives whenever we happened to meet and catch up. We bonded over our passion for sports and reminisced about our lives back home. We were two country boys living vastly different lives. He'd completed several tours in the Middle East and had been working overseas contracts for several years. After the birth of their daughter, he and his wife Somchai moved to Arkansas where his wife had chosen to live due to the large Thai community. David immediately fell in love with Arkansas. We talked about it, and he even compared it to where we grew up. He said it was small town country living. He suggested I consider making it my home as well. I think deep down he just wanted his buddy back so we could bond over college football. I was eager for a change, and I was up for a change of scenery. I checked around at my company and looked for positions in Little Rock, Arkansas. It wasn't long before I found a position as a driver and one as inside sales. Driving was not interesting to me, so I called them and inquired about the sales. The hiring manager was able to schedule me for an interview in a week. I arrived in Arkansas the Saturday before my interview to check out the place and David was right. It did remind me of being back home. He lived just 30 minutes outside of the metropolitan area and showed me around trying to sell me on the city's greatness. Little did he know that I'd already decided to make the move.

I showed up for my interview early as usual and killed it! They were impressed with my personality and business acumen. It was in the bag. I left the interview knowing they'd be reaching out to me. A few days later they called to offer me the position. I accepted and off to Arkansas I went. The owner of the house I was renting from was one of the greatest guys I knew, he reminded me of my granddaddy. We instantly clicked. One day while he was collecting the rent. He asked me to meet him at one of his buildings, not too far from where I resided, so I hung up and went over to him straight away. I got there and knocked on the door and tried looking through the window before he yelled, "Come on in."

I immediately continued to look around as I was talking and handing him my rent. He said he would get me a receipt later because he didn't have the book on him. He seemed preoccupied.

I said, "No problem, what is this place?"

He stated it had been a restaurant prior to closing. Before I could even gather my thoughts, I blurted out, "How much would you rent it to me for?"

He said, "Well $500 and $500 deposit."

I said, "I'll take it," not having plans for it, but I couldn't beat the price and the location.

He said, "Since you are renting from me I will waive the deposit."

This was a no-brainer for me. I could find something to do with this space, I was sure of it. Every day after work I took a tablet, and I went from store to store throughout town piecing together a plan for the type of business I'd do here. Having owned businesses and taking business courses at school, I was well aware of the risk of owning a restaurant, which is what I was leaning toward. Taking a risk defines entrepreneurship. That was me in a nutshell. There were considerations, such as the demographics and location, and there were restrictions on selling and serving alcohol in the county, but I wanted to go a different route. I was going with my gut on this one. I decided to go with a sports grill that didn't sell alcohol, catering to kids and families. I launched it a few weeks later, and it was a huge success. All was going well until I received that phone call about my father having stage four cancer and a short life expectancy, so I decided that family was more important. I couldn't trust running a small business from afar, so I shut it down, sold everything, and headed back to Georgia.

9

Arkansas
Online Dating (Her)

Dating sites seemed so impersonal even though they claimed to connect you on a deeper level, to find your true match, to help you navigate the sea where fish are plenty. This time I decided I do something that I hadn't done before, this time I'd be true to myself, and this time I vowed would be my last time. What I quickly realized was that really they were just the same as every other dating site. Creating algorithms by having you answer a multitude of questions and uploading attractive pictures. It's a numbers game, but since I knew this going in I said, "Okay I'll play the numbers game." I decided I'd give it the same amount of dedication and time that I would give finding a job. I checked it in the morning before work and sent some email responses. Then when I came back in the evening I would check the emails, respond to some more, and look through the profiles to see if there were any that were to my liking, and by that I meant if they were handsome or not. In the beginning I would read every profile and really make a concerted effort to respond to everyone that reached out to me, but after a while that got to be too much because I noticed that they weren't reading my profile. That was fine with me. I didn't feel bad for just looking at photos. I had my system down pat after a couple of weeks, I viewed pictures first. I weeded them out quickly. If they wore hats in every picture, I assumed they were bald...next. If they didn't smile big enough to show some teeth, I assumed they were toothless... next. If they only had pictures of themselves with sunglasses on, I assumed they were cockeyed....next. Then I'd look at the height, I theorized that men lied about their height like women lie about our weight. Anyone shorter than 5'6" was deleted. Next came their age, I gave a five year difference either way. And last I'd see if they were local, and if they were I would reach out. If they responded we had a conversation, if they were interesting enough then I would offer my phone number, and if they decided to call I would hear their voice and listen for anything that was not to the norm. I would proceed and offer to meet somewhere in public in the middle of the day where nothing was expected of either of us.

Of the many dates I went on, the most notable was Carlo. He described himself as tall (he wasn't), dark (somewhat), and handsome (very, very subjective). We met for lunch and he came with candy and a teddy bear in hand, I was impressed by the sweet gesture. Almost immediately

I knew there was no romance, and I guess that freed me to be myself and relax. We had a lot in common. We were both Puerto Rican, we had been to the same places and were looking to find someone to love. As the conversation went on, I learned that at 45 years old Carlo lived with his sister, owed $100,000 in back child support, and had been in prison three times because of it! I was in disbelief. Any one of those by themselves I could have overlooked, but all of them? There was no way. He looked so sad as he told me. We finished our lunch; I gave him a hug and said, "See you later." Even though I knew I'd never see him again.

Next up was Steven. He was nice in all of his emails. He was pleasant, he used full sentences that were punctuated correctly, and he seemed interested in what I was thinking. We exchanged numbers and spoke on the phone several times before agreeing to meet in person. He was tall, attractive, smart, and had beautiful teeth. After our drinks arrived everything went south as he casually asked me, "So have you ever dated a felon?" I thought, He couldn't be serious! Could he? Hoping he was just trying to get a reaction out of me I said, "Not that I've known, are you a felon?" He said, "Yes, I did four years in the penitentiary." I fought really hard to not show any expression in my face, but I could feel my palms start to sweat and I responded, "Hmmm, very interesting." He said he thought he told me that, but I assured him he had not. I reasoned if he was in the pen for murder he wouldn't be out, right? I knew that there were A LOT of awful things that could turn into felonies so rather than guess I asked him. I could tell he *wanted to explain. Thankfully he'd been arrested on drug charges. This led him to his next question. Had I ever dated an addict? At that moment our sandwiches had arrived, and in an effort to keep it light and be funny I jokingly asked, "Are you going to tell me you're addicted to food?" He looked at me through his glasses and after a long sigh told me he was addicted to crack cocaine. Jesus, Mary, and Joseph! He thought he told me about it during one of our many phone conversations. Once again, I assured him he had not. In his defense, he did go on to tell me that he was 12 years sober but still considered himself an addict. He laid both hands on the table and in sadness said he understood if I wanted to leave at that moment, but I didn't want to leave. What I wanted to do was give him a big hug and tell him that everything would be okay. I wasn't going to see him again. I'd already decided that when he told me he was a felon, but I was sure he'd be okay. We continued our meal in pleasant conversation. We told of each other's lives, our hopes and dreams for the future, and I learned that he had aspirations of being a drug treatment counselor, and I urged him to pursue that in earnest. Maybe what he'd been through was training for what he wanted to do. Maybe our meeting was the push he needed to start. For me the date served as a learning tool. I needed to ask more questions, and then I thought, do I really need to ask if my potential dates were drug addicts or felons?*

Undeterred, I continued in my search and came across an email I'd received several days back. His name was Devin and he wanted to know if I'd be interested in meet-

ing a hard-working, mature, attractive, Puerto Rican. Why yes! I said out loud, and I happily responded to him. Not being one to assume, I asked if he was referring to himself. He probably thought I wasn't too bright because he responded with laughing emojis. I explained that one can never be too sure on a dating website. It is better to ask questions for greater clarity. We laughed about it and went on corresponding. The next day he wrote me another message and asked if he could call me after he got off work so he could hear my voice. I gave him my phone number and said I'd be expecting his call that evening.

When he finally called, I was pleasantly surprised. He had a deep, sensuous voice that I'm sure he used to his advantage. He also spoke Spanish fluently, which I guessed helped him greatly on the dating scene. We talked for a couple of hours and sent pictures back and forth as we talked. I asked him to send me a picture of him smiling so I could see his pearly whites, but he ignored me. I saw this as not quite a red flag but more of an alert. He was 10 years divorced with three grown sons, he was a Navy vet, and a retired police officer. When we met for lunch, I couldn't get a good enough look in his mouth to see if he was missing any teeth. He didn't smile and I noticed that when he laughed, he'd either cover his mouth or laugh with his mouth closed. I'd seen that action before and that usually meant that someone either had disgusting gross teeth or missing teeth. When he talked, he tilted his face down or slightly to the side, so I was struggling to look in his mouth the whole time. For me, that was another alert. Something was going on, but

I couldn't be sure. When we finished he walked me to my car. He had a nice relaxed carefree gait that gave him an air of confidence. He was nice and all, but I wasn't too sure if I wanted a second date with him since I wasn't able to determine the status of his dental health. Did he have some kind of phobia that kept him from seeing a dentist? Did he take medicine that damaged his teeth? Did he have a vitamin deficiency? I was at a loss as to why he wouldn't show me his teeth. It was just then that I realized...I was shallow, and I did NOT feel bad about it. I didn't want to pretend that his teeth, or lack thereof, didn't bother me and then end up being in a relationship with bad teeth. I knew I couldn't get over this. I mean, if his teeth were rotted or if they were missing, why had he not replaced them with dentures or had them repaired? After all, he was in the Navy for a while and was a retired policeman! Surely his previous employers offered dental plans?! To me that was indicative of some deeper problem. I had to be sure before I made a decision, so when he said he wanted to go out with me again I accepted. I gave him a quick hug goodbye and got in my car. It turns out that he was smarter than I gave him credit for. I was thinking that our second date would be outside in the bright light of day so I could make him talk and laugh a lot, then I'd be able to get a good look in his mouth. Unfortunately for me he took me to a comedy show, at night, and of course we had to sit in the darkest corner. Again I tried in vain to see if I could make out any teeth, but I figured out that he'd mastered the art of barely moving his lips when he spoke, and it didn't help that the comic was not particularly funny that night. I was done. I knew that short of me asking him to open his mouth and say "ahh" there was not much I could do to really be 100% sure. When the evening was over I said goodnight, evaded him when he tried to kiss me, and said "see you later", knowing full well I was never going to call him again. There were various false starts, prospects that would reach out and after I would answer, I'd never hear from them again. At one point I felt like I'd seen all the eligible men in Arkansas. I was starting to lose hope. I persisted, not just because I was stubborn, but because I knew my better half was out there and I didn't want to quit without knowing I'd given it my all. I prayed for patience and kept scrolling.

I'd been in Arkansas for about a year, and I was glad that I wasn't disappointed. Yes, for being the capital city it was a little sleepy. Yes, the people were a little long-winded and tended to visit a little more than I was used to, but that's one of the reasons I wanted to leave Los Angeles. I wanted to leave Los Angeles because I wanted to wake up to the sounds of birds singing outside my window not police sirens and helicopters. I had to remind myself that I wasn't in the big city anymore. When I had a doctor's appointment or meeting in Los Angeles I had to learn to arrive early just to be on time. It wasn't until I came to Arkansas that I understood the meaning of "country time". I'd arrive early for a staff meeting only to have to sit around and visit until everyone else showed up. The facilitator would usually start with "let's give everyone time to arrive." The city girl inside me wanted to scream! What do you mean? They should *have arrived 15 minutes ago when the meeting started. The newfound country girl in me held me back and said, "Girl, you've got to relax." So I did. Appointment times I learned, were just a suggestion. Driving was a different experience altogether. Driving into town, the GPS alerted me to some heavy traffic. I looked out across the four-lane highway and I saw five cars in front of me. I was prepared for the heavy traffic I'd grown used to in Los Angeles, but I was pleasantly surprised to see it was only those four cars. The benefits of moving to a small town for me greatly outweighed the drawbacks. I had the nature, less congestion with less traffic, free parking spaces. I felt I could breathe. So what if I couldn't buy liquor on Sundays? I only had to be told no ma'am once at the grocery store to learn. As I pulled out my identification card, thinking that the cashier thought that I was underage, she went on to explain that it was Sunday and they weren't allowed to sell wine on Sundays. So what if I couldn't take my car to the shop or go to the mall later in the day on Sunday. I learned Sundays were for God and family. I also found out that being from the city meant I was a heathen and I must need Jesus because all of a sudden everyone wanted to pray for me. I thought it was hilarious that my exasperation was met with a solemn "bless your heart." I learned I had to have more patience and anticipate that my new winged friends would be singing outside my window way before I was ready to wake up. I often heard the saying the early bird catches the worm but really!? No one is up that early, not even the worm. And on the upside, I could count on traffic delays lasting minutes not* hours, and a little extra time before meetings to visit with my co-workers and new best friends was never a bad thing. As I was dutifully checking my emails one night, I opened the one from him. His profile said he was interested in "Networking". I thought it was odd to put that on a dating site, but I'd seen stranger things. He lived in Little Rock, was an entrepreneur, he was handsome, and single. I was drafting an email to him when his name lit up to indicate that he was also online. He sent me an instant message and we started a conversation. I liked that he had a sense of humor. He had recently had a birthday. I wished him a happy birthday and it turns out it was one day before mine. We talked about our jobs and our families and after a couple of hours we logged off and promised to log back on the next day. After work, I got back on the site and started viewing some profiles when I saw his name light up again. I instantly messaged him, and we chatted for another hour. This time before I logged off, I gave him my phone number and let him know he could either call or text.

I didn't have to wait long for him to text me, and I was glad. After work he called me, and we had a long conversation. I liked the sound of his voice. He had such a thick country accent that I had to ask him to repeat himself several times. I liked that he was funny and seemed genuine. When he asked if I was open to meeting him for coffee I agreed. We would meet in two days at Barnes and Noble after work. I didn't want to expect too much, but I was hoping it would go well. In the meantime, we called each other and texted. My profile had current pictures, so I let him know that I looked the same, there would be no surprises. I made sure when I got ready for work that morning I wore something that accentuated my best features, and when the day came I got a call from him a couple of hours before the date. He wanted to reschedule our date, move the time up, something about being available right then. I was a little surprised. I was still at work and there was no way I could leave early, so I told him I couldn't meet earlier but if he wanted to reschedule for another day we could. But he said it was fine and he'd meet me in a couple of hours. I made sure to freshen up my make-up and dabbed a little bit of perfume before I headed to the bookstore. When I got there, I texted him and let him know I'd be by the magazines. I wish I could say that I saw fireworks or stars or something telling like that, but I didn't. I just saw him walking towards me and it felt like I'd known him already. He was a little shorter than I was used to, but he was handsome, polite, and when he smiled his whole face lit up. And his teeth? They were absolutely perfect. We introduced ourselves and found a place to sit. Our conversation wasn't awkward or forced. I felt at ease and comfortable. We didn't run out of things to say, and I found myself asking him questions just so I could hear his country accent. After a couple of hours, I heard that closing time had arrived and we made an official date for 2 days later, on Saturday.

We stepped out on faith believing that what we'd done in the past to attract a mate was not going to work for the long term. He wasn't interested in one-night stands. His preference was a product of being in the streets, hustling and grinding. He'd left a trail of broken hearts. All of them complete with smooth, toned thighs, firm, round derrieres, and melted chocolate complexions. Beauties by anybody's standards. For me building a profile on a dating site helped me to realize that as much as I hated to admit it, I was shallow. Throughout all of my adult life I'd been attracted to the classically tall, dark, strong, and handsome ones. My motto was "If he can't pick me up, he cannot pick me up!" None of that had worked for me, it just led to a bunch of a lonely nights. Yes, I went out on a lot of dates, but I came up empty. If anybody lasted more than 6 months they might be happy to have sex with me, but no one wanted to marry me. Apparently, I just wasn't the type.

10

Arkansas
Online Dating (Him)

I found myself back in Arkansas after getting an offer from my employer that I could not refuse: expense account, company car, living allowance, and moving expenses all paid. I would be a fool to pass it up. I really wasn't too keen on returning back to Arkansas, but I wanted to open myself up to the Universe and anything that might come my way.

I was very excited to be in a place in my life where I could really focus on my love life. I felt great and according to my doctor my health was exactly where it should be. I looked good and my confidence was high. I was at the top of my career, number one in the nation in outside sales with my company! My commission was unbelievable. The only thing that was missing was that very special someone, that one that completes you. Everything was falling into place for me as it usually does. I had plenty of time to dedicate to finding someone that I could live the rest of my life with. Some of my co-worker's wives and girlfriends tried to set me up on a few blind dates. I was ready and receptive for whatever came my way, so I geared up for what I knew would be the first of many. I'm lucky the good Lord blessed me with charm, finesse, and good looks because at 5ft 7in, he definitely shorted me on height. Not the shortest, but certainly not the tallest in the crowd.

Mornings seemed to come faster and faster every morning. "All the way up" remix with Fat Joe woke me up at 4am. Even though it was still dark outside and the old me would have just hit the snooze and rolled over, my commitment to myself helped get me out of bed and into the shower. Not long ago I decided enough was enough! I wanted to be healthy, so I changed my diet and implemented 6-7 days of cardio and weights and lost 68 pounds. I vowed after 3 years still at it #nevergoingback. As I started my daily routine of hopping in the shower to wake me up, I grabbed my phone and clicked one of my online dating apps. The icon was normally lit up with several messages. Let me see what shenanigans will be waiting in my inbox I said to myself. I opened up my messages and sifted through the unappealing exterior ones. After quickly doing so, I skimmed through their profiles. I looked for particular things that stood out. Is the look right? Does she look like she's covering something? Is there a full body picture? Is she in my age range? Is she in the area? Then I started to narrow it down a little more. Is she a smoker? Does she drink?

Does she love the Lord? Does she have young children? I reached out to a few with a "Good Morning" and then waited patiently. Usually by the time I was done with my workout I had plenty of responses to keep me busy. I headed to the gym and as I jumped on the elliptical, I heard a "bing". I looked at my notifications and someone had responded with a "Good Morning" back.

"How was your night?"

"It was great! Thank you for asking. And how was yours?"

"It was okay, but morning came too quick."

This went on for most of my workout. We chatted about work and about her kids. One was in college and another was a senior in high school. She said she worked for an independent lottery and radio company. All was going well until she said she was living with her parents. I was a bit apprehensive, but we proceeded, exchanged numbers, and decided to meet up.

I drove up to her house, she came out and got in the truck. Being a non-smoker I immediately smelled cigarettes even though she was not smoking. I asked her, "Do you smoke?" She said, "Yes, is that a problem?" I smiled half-heartedly and said, "No, as long it is not around me." I immediately knew I wasn't feeling her. We sat in the truck and continued to talk a little bit more. When we ended our conversation, I dropped her off and headed home. The next morning she texted.

"Good Morning."

"Good Morning."

Then all of a sudden, she started ranting about her employer having financial issues and how she might not get paid. Then she went on about her ex-husband and how he is in jail and not paying child support. I was listening, but the whole time I was thinking, "Why is she telling me all this so early?" I didn't feel like having that conversation with someone I just met, so I apologized and let her know she could call me later when she felt a little better. I found out bright and early the next morning.

"Good morning, may I get $10 for gas?" I was embarrassed for her. I am well aware that people go through situations, but $10?

"If you stopped smoking cigarettes, you'd have more than the $10 you are asking me for."

I know it sounded calloused, but I was getting a real glimpse of her as a person, and I wasn't interested. At this point I was just trying to be a good listener, but I also informed her that I refused to support a habit that is not mine and not healthy to boot! She started going off! I mean she was pissed and said,

"You can't let me get $10 dollars?"

"It's definitely not the money, it's the principal of the matter."

"I don't need another bill in my life" I decided that was not the best situation for me. I hung up and never talked to her again.

April was the next lady that I met online. She was a vast improvement. She had braces, which made her quirky, and a nice physique. We went out a couple times. Everything seemed to be heading in a positive direction and I was feeling hopeful. Emotions escalated! So one day we were on what was becoming our regular phone calls and she said, "I want to tell you two things, and

I have been wanting to tell you this since day one." I was curious. What could she have to tell me since day one? I didn't have a clue what was about to come out her mouth. She said, "One, I'm an ordained minister, and 2nd, would you like to come to my trial sermon?" I was taken aback. With my strong religious upbringing I was thinking, "Oh my God, I'm going straight to Hell." Not just for the fornication aspect, but for being with an ordained minister. I was somewhat of a womanizer, and I answered to no one. I'd been told I was a handsome devil and that I was Satan himself, yet I would never peg her for being an ordained minister. Why couldn't I see that? Was I blinded by my lust? Or was God using her to get to me? I didn't know and I didn't care to figure it out. We discussed everything and for a moment my mind was at ease. We continued to date and one day we went out and had a great night of drinking and enjoying each other. We went back to her place and before we realized it time had gotten away from us. She said, "It is really late, so you should just crash here tonight and then leave tomorrow." Going against my better judgment I conceded and said, "Ok, that will work." I jumped in the shower and climbed in the bed.

One thing led to another and more hours has passed. We laid there together, her head resting on my chest telling how much she was in love with me and how she knew God was going to work everything out for us. I must have dozed off because the next thing I knew I heard voices chanting over me and in my stupor I said to myself, "Am I dreaming?" I was disoriented and quickly realized I was not in the comfort of my own bed. I forced myself awake and realized that it was not a dream. I looked up and saw April standing over me with a crazy look in her eyes. She seemed to be in deep prayer or maybe a trance. I'd never seen this side of her before. I heard her praying, but it sounded like mumbling and in her hand, she held a bottle. My first thought was "Is she about to end my life? What did I do wrong?" I felt something on my face. I slowly moved my hand to wipe my face and she grabbed it. I thought she had hit me and I was bleeding. I began to get angry. I jerked my hand away and went to wipe my face more aggressively while staring her down. I looked down at my hand expecting to see blood, but all that was there was a thick oily substance. Had I been anointed in my sleep? I was getting more confused and upset by the minute. I said, "What in the world are you doing?" She quickly blurted out, "I am not trying to hurt you, I was just placing holy oil on you and praying for you that the lord would allow you see how we were meant to be together." Then she crouched low to the bed and put her face close to mine and continued "…and he would cast out all the lustful spirits out of you." I couldn't believe what I was hearing. I wondered, "Is this what if feels like to be crazy?" I got up and proceeded to the bathroom while looking over my shoulder the whole time. I got up real close to the mirror and saw that sure enough, this crazy woman had smeared an oily mess that vaguely looked like a cross all over my forehead. I grabbed a washcloth and wiped my face clean. I went back in the bedroom without saying a word. This was my fault; I had no words. I put my clothes on, headed downstairs, got in my car, asked the good Lord to forgive me for corrupting one of his chosen ones, and drove home. That would be last time I would ever go back to that house again.

A few weeks later I logged back on a couple of the dating sites, and I was pleasantly surprised when I came across a beautifully interesting profile. As I read it, I hoped that it was a real person and that I wasn't being "Catfished", so after hesitating for a couple of moments I decided to send her a brief message in hopes of getting a response and breaking the ice. A week or so later I looked in my inbox and saw that I had received a message from her with interest and after I gave her profile a good once over, I said, are you local? Are you single? Do you have children? It seemed like I was cutting and pasting the same questions to everyone that I interacted with. Frankly it was getting a little tedious, and I was frustrated. But I was interested in this one, something about her made me want to reach out. After a brief email exchange, we decided to meet for coffee and a little bit of conversation at a local bookstore. We set a date, three days away. And the time, after 5pm. I had to admit I was excited and feeling a little hopeful. In the meantime, we called each other and texted often. When the day came, I found that I had finished my meetings early and had about two, maybe three hours of free time to kill. I decided to call her and see if we could push up our time.

"Would it be okay if we met up a little earlier?"

"I'm sorry, I'm still at work," she said, "but if you can't make it, it's okay we can reschedule for another day."

Noticing her apprehension, I said, "No, no, it's ok. It's not a problem. I'll see you in a few hours."

I felt something in my spirit telling me that she was worth waiting for. One never knows how the online meeting will go. You just pray you won't become a victim of a "Catfishing" scam. So when I called Neida to reschedule an earlier time for our meeting at Barnes and Noble and she told me she couldn't meet earlier but we could reschedule "if I liked", I told her I would just wait and work on following up with work emails, but what I was really doing was surfing all the other dating sites on my phone. Still searching and hoping to find "The One", especially if she turned out not to be "The One".

I was in the parking lot scrolling and sitting, waiting for a call or text from her to let me know she had arrived when the phone rang. I answered, "Hello, you must be here!" Having lost track of time and anticipating that she was calling to reschedule. She said in her sexy voice, "I'm inside." I said, "Whaaattt!! How did you slip past me? I'm on my way in." She said, "Ok, I'm at the magazine section." I hurried and as I got out of my truck I thought to myself: "Goddammit, how did I miss her?" I detested being late. I saw it more as a character flaw than just a simple personality trait. When she texted me to let me know she was already there I got a little angry at myself. If this meeting went south I didn't want it to be because of me. I walked in and walked toward the magazines turning a couple corners. I saw the breathtaking lady sitting on the bench with glasses on and her hair pulled back and a smile that lit up a room. I must have been mesmerized by her eyes because 3 hours later we both looked up as we heard an announcement that the Barnes and Noble would be closing in 10 minutes.

"Please make your final selections and proceed to the front for purchase." We both immediately looked at each other and both laughed.

"Wow!" I said.

"OMG!" she said. "Time has definitely got away from us."

We talked about so much. It seemed like I had already known her, so I suggested we have an official date early on Saturday. Lunch and a movie. Since I didn't like to go to the movies late, plus matinees and the lunch menu are always half price, it would be a win/win. Between Thursday and Saturday, we texted and talked often. I didn't know what she was thinking, but I definitely knew what I was thinking. I was thinking, "What a breath of fresh air chatting with such an intellectual woman." I had no idea that I'd just the woman that I'd make my wife.

11

Arkansas
1st Date (Her)

It was Saturday and I'd rushed in to work super early that morning because there was something pressing that required my attention. I was alone in the office with no distractions, so I put on some soft music, and before I knew it, it was 11:30 and I got a text on my phone from Marcel.

"Hi pretty lady," he said. "Would you like to meet up somewhere, or would you like me to pick you up?"

I looked at the text and panicked.

"Oh my goodness!" I texted back.

"I'm so sorry, I totally lost track of time. I'm still at work."

We'd texted the night before to coordinate a meeting time for today, but I hadn't read his whole text where he mentioned he wanted to catch a movie THEN have lunch.

I was flustered. I hoped that my slip up wouldn't discourage him, so I offered a suggestion.

"I can leave here at 12pm and be ready by 12:30. Let me know where I can meet you."

Thankfully, he responded right away.

"Ok, that will be fine, but I don't mind picking you up."

"I don't want you to go out of your way..." I texted.

"It won't be out of my way."

"Great! Then you can pick me up."

I texted him my address and hustled to wrap things up as quickly as I could while I mentally went through my closet for an appropriate outfit. Luckily, my apartment was minutes from my job, so the 30 minutes I'd given myself would be plenty of time for me to spruce up.

I got into my apartment and threw off my clothes as I ran down the hallway and into the bathroom. I got into the tub for the quickest shower in all of my adult life. Pits, ass, crack, and face, fast, fast, fast. Only slowing down to get the soap out of my eyes! I got out of the shower and dried myself off. 7 minutes great. No time to mess around, deodorant, lotion, perfume. I went to my closet and got my favorite jeans and a nice blouse, but I was still too moist to slip on the jeans, so I went back to the bathroom to comb my hair. Hair was a little damp, so I turned on the blow dryer. Ok, high heat, quick, quick, quick. No time to put on makeup or contacts. Lip balm, earrings, bracelet. Went back to my jeans, still had to bounce a couple of times to get into them but no more than any other day. Shoes, where are my shoes? I went to my shoe rack and got my cutest black flats just in case we were going to do some walking. I didn't want to worry about walking in heels. Time check,

I looked at my phone, 12:25 and a text from him appears. "I'm here."

Great, he's punctual! I text back, "Here I come, just getting my pocketbook!"

I went to my room, grabbed my pocketbook, and started frantically looking for my phone before I realized it was already in my hand. Relieved, I looked in the mirror. "Sexy Librarian" would have to do for today. I got my keys and my wallet and headed out the door.

As I locked the door, I looked over my shoulder and saw a big white truck waiting. "That must be him," I thought. I waved and started to walk toward him. As I got closer, he got out of the truck and came around to open my door.

"Pero miralo," I said, pleasantly surprised. "Hi Marcel!"

He smiled with a mouth full of healthy white teeth and responded as he helped me in.

"Hi Beautiful."

I smiled and buckled up as he went back around to get in. "I'm sorry for the miscommunication," I said. He looked at me and smiled and responded, "Don't even worry about it, just a small hiccup. Okay, so where would you like to go first?" After going back and forth about it a little bit, we decided that we would go to the movie first and then do lunch, so we went to see this new movie that was playing called Chappaquiddick. I was surprised that he would want to see that. I wanted to see it because it was about the Kennedys. He wanted to see it because it was about powerful men. We sat right in the middle of the movie theater side by side. He reached out to hold my hand early in the movie and I didn't *pull away. We held hands through the whole show. Usually my hands get clammy and sweaty right away, but this time they didn't and if they did, he didn't pull away either. We talked a little during the movie but not too much, he said he didn't want to ruin my movie experience. He whispered that he was glad that we had come to watch this movie and he was glad that he was watching it with me. When we got out of the movie theater it was still early enough that we could have lunch, so we decided to go to one of the new restaurants that had just opened up in the area. We sat at a booth and instead of sitting across from each other, I insisted that he sit right next to me so we could be much closer and it would be a little bit more intimate. I was enjoying being with him and I could tell he was enjoying being with me as well. We talked about a lot of things. We talked about our families, about how we had both been in Atlanta at the same time. We talked about what we wanted to do in the future and the types of connections we wanted to make. We talked about the dating site and how I felt that he kind of ignored me in the beginning. He told me it wasn't him ignoring me but usually he turned on his profile, looked through a couple of women, and then being disillusioned would turn his account off again. I didn't see the purpose. I told him for me I just looked constantly until I found the right one. I didn't tell him, but I felt like this was the right one. Our date lasted 7 hours. After our late lunch we went out for a walk and then he took me back home. We hugged and said we were definitely going to do this again because we both knew that we would.*

C

Love is a Place

I'm not sure when I started to look at Marcel and see the man I love. Falling in love with him was easy. I knew that I wanted to spend time with him, it didn't matter what we did. I was all in. I didn't care if he thought I was "extra" or too clingy. I wanted to be who I was and show him how important he was to me. We would talk on the phone every couple of days and I would tell him, "Oh, hi! I haven't spoken to you in such a long time." He'd look at me sideways and respond, "Golly, we just spoke 2 days ago!" It would make me crazy. When he'd call me in the mornings I'd say, "Hi, Marshmelo. I missed you so much." He'd respond, "Game."

I didn't understand and asked him, "What do you mean?"

"You saying you miss me is game." Puzzled, I'd respond, "I have no game," and he'd say,

"No game is the game." I'd just laugh it off because he didn't strike me as being insecure, but for some reason when I told him I liked him and wanted to hang out with him he was surprised.

One day after work Marcel called me asking if I had any plans after work. "No," I said, "just going home to relax."

"I'm headed to the gym to work out, would you like to come with me?" The answer in my head was, "Hell no!" I worked out every day during my lunch hour, but I hated it. I did it because I knew I had to stay healthy. When he

asked me I didn't want to right away say "no" so what I said was, "Maybe we can work out tomorrow, I wouldn't want to slow you down and mess up your routine."

He said, "You won't, I'm due for a change of pace."

I wanted to hang out with him more than I hated working out, so I conceded and he came to pick me up. This started a routine for us. From that point on, every weekday after work we'd get together, work out, and then hang out in his truck for hours, and then I'd go to my apartment and he'd go to his. Even when we got mad and argued he'd call to ask me if I wanted to work out, and then we'd talk and not be mad at each other anymore. We had our share of rough patches. He'd get mad because I wasn't committed to our relationship or because he felt I was too lackadaisical. Which was not true, he just wasn't used to the way I responded sometimes. If I forgot that I'd made plans or asked him to confirm a date he'd say, "Honey Bunches, that's suspect as hell" and refuse to see me. I'd have to coax him into understanding that I didn't have nefarious plans to juggle three and four men at the same time.

Arkansas- 1st Date (Him)

When Saturday finally came, I texted her to confirm the time and she said, "OMG!" as she frequently said. "I am at work, but I can get off at 12:30pm." I was thinking, here we go again! Should I cancel or go against my better judgement and compromise? She said she could finish up right away and suggested we go to a movie first and then have lunch. I decided to compromise and I'm glad I did; the day was perfect. The movie experience was awesome, and lunch/dinner was great. I believe in love, but love and the individual come in all forms. I wanted a woman I could build with. My buddy always said that some of the most powerful men were backed by some of the most powerful women the Lynne Cheney, Hillary Clinton, and the Michelle Obama's of the world. The list could go on and on. So after talking to her that evening at Barnes and Noble, I knew she had the potential to be what I needed her to be, I just didn't know in what capacity. I definitely wanted to find out more about her and how we could conquer the world together. Well, I discovered that I was still me with my selfish ways. I guess before I never wanted to take the time out to truly extend my love to anyone. So why start now?

Although I felt an array of emotions for this woman, her wanting to spend more time, I found myself creating many excuses why I couldn't from, "I have to work late" to "I just saw you last week!" She had a trip planned to go to the Puerto Rican festival in Chicago and had invited me to join her. I opted out on this trip. I don't know if it was because it was too soon in our relationship, or if I was just continuing with my selfish ways. Either one, the fact was that this was the turning point of our relationship for me. When she left and that one night went by, I was feeling some type of way. I thought of the saying, "You won't miss the water 'till the well runs dry." I was missing this one so much. I guess I was taking our new relationship for granted, and I didn't realize that my love had grown to feelings that I have not experienced before and was somewhat scared to embrace. I caught myself continuously looking at my phone to see if I had missed a text or had a message from her. I had never been through these feelings before and I was trying hard to dismiss them. I spoke with her every night before we went to sleep. I knew at the very moment that when she returned home, I was going to do everything in my soul to prove my love and commitment to her. I was determined to win her heart. I had a formula. Just add Marcel and you have recipe of eternal love. This was my challenge.

12

Arkansas
Yes, Back Where it Started

I knew that I wanted to be married. I knew that what I wanted in a man was one that would look at me and see someone that he could not live without. That the mere thought of being without me made him start to ache. I wanted to find that man that would choose me above all others because, although I'm not perfect, I'm perfect for him. And I wanted him to know that the love he would give me I'd give it back one hundred times. I didn't know how much I was missing or how being loved felt, but with Marcel I'm making up for lost time.

It was raining again, but we wouldn't let that stop our weekend routine. We crisscrossed the city as we hit all of our stops for running errands and finding a place to eat. Marcel tells me that his friend had been featured in a magazine and he wanted to support him by buying a couple of issues.

He'd been telling me that for the past month almost, so to know that the magazine feature was finally out was great. Excitedly I said, "Oh really, which magazine?"

"I'm not sure of the name Honey Bunches, I can call him to find out."

As he started to make a call, I asked him what store could we buy it.

"He said it's available at Barnes and Noble or Books a Million."

I reminded him that there was a Barnes and Noble just off the highway (as a matter of fact, it's the one where we first met) and I got on my phone to see their hours. "Ok, they are open until 7pm tonight so we should head out before it starts raining any harder," I said. When we got to the bookstore Marcel let me off in the front and said, "Go to the magazine section and sit and wait for me Honey Bunches." I heard him, but I was confused as to why he was being so specific. How did he want me to look for the magazine if I was sitting down? Nonplussed, I walked over to the magazine section and I was going to sit down but all the chairs were put up, so I walked over to the racks to look for the magazine. I wasn't sure the name of the magazine or what the feature was about, but he told me it might have been "High Times". As I started to look Marcel came over and said, "What are you doing Honey Bunches?"

"I'm looking for the magazine, but I don't see it, what was the name?

"Ok, I'm not sure. Let me run to the restroom first."

As he said that he was off and I stayed looking for the magazine, still not able to see it, I was going to walk over to the service desk, but since he told me to stay by the magazines I took out my phone instead. I was getting ready to call the service desk when Marcel walked out. As he walked up to me he said, "It's not about a magazine, Babe." I was intent on finding this magazine and I heard him, but I really wasn't paying attention, we had to find this magazine. I kept looking and he said, "You know I love you Honey Bunches."

"Yes, MarshMelo. I know. I love you too."

"We're going to be together for the rest of our lives...."

"Yes, Baby. That's the plan, we're doing it!"

Still looking for the magazine he said, "I have one thing I want to say to you."

I looked at him and laughed because he was mimicking one of our favorite comedians. "What do you have to say to me?"

Then I saw him crouch low and I thought he had found the magazine, so I started to get low next to him. He pushed me and motioned for me to stay up. He got down on one knee. Now I was thoroughly confused.

Then he held the black velvet box open and said, "Will you make me the happiest man in the world and be my wife?"

I was baffled! All I could say was, "What, are you serious?"

I couldn't believe it. I was trying to untangle the mess in my brain. I looked at the ring and it was perfect, beau-

tiful, and exactly what I had wanted. So many thoughts
were racing through my head, but I just said, "WHAT?!?"
He told me we were going to look for engagement rings
next week. When and how did he plan all this? He was
looking at me with that big smile full of white teeth that
I loved so much, and he bought me back to my senses.

"You still haven't said Yes Honey Bunches."

"Oh My Gosh, Yes, Yes! Of course, yes!"

He stood up and I kissed him and hugged him tight.
I kept thinking how I never thought it would happen to
me. To find that one person that wanted to spend the
rest of their life with me was something that I always
knew I wanted. To be loved and give love right back.
It's what movies and songs are written about but wasn't
sure it would ever happen to me. To know that someone
had chosen ME was a gift. To have it be someone I love
was more that I could imagine. All I could do was cry.

I had grown to love this man, I loved that I wanted to
spend every moment with him, and I loved that he let me be
silly and corny and didn't refuse when I made him be silly
and corny too. I loved that he made me laugh. I loved that
he couldn't keep his hands off me and that he didn't even
pull away when I wanted to hold him close. I never knew
what a love like this would feel like. It took me zigzagging
all over the place to finally find my cowboy. I found him,
and I was keeping him because we loved and respected each
other, and our love was greater than the two of us. We
had generations of love moving us along in the right path.

$\mathcal{C}\mathrm{\gamma}$

DNA Test– Arkansas

It was a typical Saturday morning in Arkansas for us. No work, no alarm clock, nothing but our internal clocks to wake us up. She's not an early riser, so I reached over and gently laid my hand on her hips and ass since that is one of her characteristics that I fell in love with and gently coaxed her awake.

She moaned softly and with her morning raspy voice said, "Mmm, good morning Melo."

We'd kept the nicknames we had given each other since the very beginning of the relationship. I called her "Honey Bunches of Oats" since she had that beautiful golden complexion and mouth tasted like honey. She called me MarshMelo but often shortened it to Melo because she said under my tough exterior, I was all sweet and soft like a marshmallow.

I said, "Good morning Honey Bunches".

"Buenos dias My MarshMelo," she responded.

We grabbed our phones to check our schedules for the day, a rarity, nothing planned for us. We were newlyweds only being married for three months. Our professional lives were so busy that we had decided to get married at the Justice of the Peace and had a small reception with only family and a couple of friends. Enjoying the rarity of the morning and the pleasure of her lying next to me, I could not believe how perfect we were for each other. We promised we would plan a honeymoon at a later date. And as we laid in bed with her head on my chest we talked about our options for the day. She kicked the sheets off of her, got up quickly, and ran to the den.

"Where you going Honey Bunches?"

"Esperate, real quick," she responded as she ran into the room.

"...Oh hold on, I forgot to tell you."

When she came back, she was waving two packages in the air and as she held them up she said in a sing-song voice, "Guess what these are?" giggling and looking so accomplished.

I laughed as she hopped back into bed with both packages, handing one to me and said, "Here, one for you and one for me."

"Well, what are they?"

"It's our DNA tests, all we have to do is put a little bit of spit in the tube and mail it back! And then... " she went on building the anticipation, "When it comes back in about 4 to 6 weeks we will know exactly where we're from!"

Pretending to be exhausted and winded, she laid next to me and started to explain like she was a schoolteacher.

"You know how we talked about how cool it would be to know the history and origins of our families?"

"Yes, Honey Bunches, I remember."

I responded and laughed because it was at times like these, when she had this innocence and childlike wonderment about her, that I was reminded of how much I love her.

"Well, this is how we're going to do it."

We opened the packages and started reading the instructions. It was very simple, just put a couple of drops of saliva into the tube that was provided and put it into the self-addressed, stamped envelope. She straightened up, reached over, and grabbed the laptop from the nightstand.

"We have to register each one too. Let's do that now so we don't forget."

After reading the literature and registering both the tests, she exclaimed, "In 4-6 weeks we will have our answers, isn't that awesome?"

I nodded in agreement and reached over to hug her tight.

"I love you woman."

"I love you too Melo, so much."

She put the laptop back on the nightstand and threw the sheet over us. As we lay under the sheet I grabbed her face in my hands and I was taken aback by the love I felt for her. For the first time in my life I could say that I loved someone and felt that she loved me. I felt an overwhelming urge to make love to her.

The feel of her bare skin against mine sent chills up and down my spine. Every time we touched it felt like small bursts of electricity. I looked into her eyes that were like rich, dark pools of Puerto Rican coffee and saw love reflected in them. I closed my eyes and inhaled the scent of her body and let it fill my nostrils as it took me to a place of pure joy. I wanted to give her the world and took joy in experiencing new things with her. How could a person so unassuming and down to earth bring out a feeling in me that I didn't know I had? Deciding not to ponder it any longer, I accepted this gift that life had given me. I wrapped her in my arms, held her close to me, and whispered in her ear as I made love to her over and over again.

$\backsim$

I was at work when I got a notification that my DNA results had come in, so I excitedly logged into the website to finally see where my ancestors from. Every time Papi and I would talk about our people in Africa he would only say "Africa" he would never identify a specific region. I had done some research on my own and found that there were a lot of tribes from Nigeria that had been taken to Puerto Rico during the time when Spain had control of the island. I had even advised some friends that I was from Nigeria, so I was thoroughly surprised to learn that I was ethnically Cameroonian, Congolese, and Southern Bantu, as well as Spanish and Portuguese. I immediately called Marcel to let him know my news.

"Guess what Melo?"

"What is it Honey Bunches?"

"I'm Cameroonian!" I was super excited that the pieces were all coming together, and he responded,

"Are you serious? Baby, I'm Cameroonian too!" We began to compare our percentages and he laughed at how Nigeria was way at the bottom of my list.

"Dangit, Honey Bunches, what if we're related?" I laughed at him and said, "No way Babe. My Africans were taken to Puerto Rico and never left. Your Africans made it to Georgia." It was unmistakable that we were in for an adventure as we were both determined to find out what our connection was.

$\mathcal{C}\sim$

Homeland

Our flight landed and we descended into Cameroon. I had managed to look at some maps and read up on the country, and I was eager to see all the places that I had only read about. Marcel and Thomas were still talking, and I looked up from my book to hear Marcel explain,

"What happened was that every time I found myself in Atlanta, I missed her by a couple of days."

Thomas reiterated to get a better understanding, "So, she got to Atlanta, was there for a while then left. You missed her by a day or two?"

"Yes," said Marcel, "exactly."

"Okay, then you left Georgia for school, but came back for your granddaddy. Meanwhile Neida had gone to California for her daddy."

I nodded, and Marcel closed his eyes in satisfaction and said, "You got it brother."

"Then you left Georgia to go to Arkansas and you were there for a while, and then your father got sick and you left. Neida then goes to Arkansas, just missing you by a month or two."

"That's right!" We all raised our hands and congratulated ourselves. Feeling accomplished, we all sat back.

"Man, what a journey," Thomas said.

"Yes, Sir it is," Marcel said.

"And it brings us to now," I said.

c͡

The long flight finally came to an end. Chatting with Thomas throughout the flight about our lives made the trip bearable. We were finally here: Cameroon, Africa.

It was all like a dream. A place that I didn't think I would ever be. I was looking forward to meeting Neida's family and before we could get off the plane there they were, holding up cute signs saying, "Welcome Family." We were welcomed with hugs and kisses from all of the family. They grabbed our bags and escorted us to their car. We were on the main highway for a bit, then we went down several dirt roads past many wilds animals. Well, to us they seemed wild. To them it must have been just a regular nuisance, like a deer or a raccoon on the roads back home. It seemed like we were on safari in an episode on the National Geographic Channel. We finally arrived to a community of small houses. Everyone threw their arms up and said, "Our home is your home." I looked over at Neida and as always in situations like this, her eyes were full of tears. I said, "Are you OK? What's wrong?" She said nothing as always, but I knew she was shaken up by the love she was being shown by family she had never met. More love shown than by family she had known all her life. So we stopped at one of the houses. Several of the elderly women were watching and waving. As we stopped, they embraced us and showered us with more hugs and kisses. Tears began to be shed by various if not all of the people in the small crowd. You could feel the wave of emotions as we walked through the crowd into the house. We were offered something to drink and eat. We both took cold drinks and they asked what we'd like to do first. My wife said, "I want to know everything about my family here. As far as anyone can date back." At that very moment a young boy came walking up to us with what appeared to be a large book. He could barely hold it up as he extended his arms out to give it to Neida.

"What is this handsome young man?"

A voice shouted out from the crowd, "It's a photo album. It's our history, your history."

I grabbed it for her, and we sat down together on the couch. We started from the beginning. An elderly lady, Serah, described each person in the photograph and told a story about every picture. Who it was and how they were related to us. Neida came to a picture of a beautiful woman that stunned her. For the first time, the elderly lady didn't have anything to say.

Neida smiled at her and asked, "Who is this? Who is this lady that looks so much like me?"

I saw it for myself. It was like looking at her twin sister if she had one. Everyone was quiet.

Serah looked at us with her wrinkly face and softly said, "That is your great-great-great grandmother."

All I heard was "OMG! WOW! I wish I could have met her."

Once again everyone was quiet. We looked around watching everyone's reactions and no one wanted to look us in the eyes.

I said, "What is wrong, why the silence?"

A young lady blurted out, "She is still living!"

It was our turn to be silent for a moment.

Neida looked at me quizzically and said softly, "Could this be true? Could my great-great-great grandmother Lusamba still be living?"

That meant that would make her over 100 years old!

Serah said, "This is true. She left the village years ago, even before I was born, with a broken heart and told everyone to let her be and made everyone promise never to come to seek her out."

I said that we would really love to see her. They explained that they would arrange to have one of the male family members go to check on her periodically to see if she was still living. They don't go to her bungalow, but they look from afar to see if she comes out and goes back in. Then they come back to report her condition.

I asked, "Can you take us there?"

"We can't," she said. "We promised her."

I said, "You asked what we would like, and that is what we want."

Serah said, "We will do this. We will lead you in the direction to her bungalow, and from there you will be on your own."

I said, "That's all we ask."

We were led as close as they would take us and said, "You would have to travel the rest of the way on feet."

So we traveled, enduring the heat and insects. We came upon this small bungalow, and as we walked up to the door to knock, the door opened, slowly and carefully. There stood this small, beautiful, old lady with a machete in her hand. We stood there both with eyes and mouths wide open and stuck in our tracks. She dropped the machete and stared at Neida for what seemed like forever. She reached for her slowly, then she looked at me and grabbed my face and gave me a huge hug and a kiss on my cheeks.

I held her hands in mine and said, "This is your great-great-great-granddaughter." She shook her head "yes" as if she was saying, "I know! I know!" Her voice was gravely and thick with an accent. She invited us in and asked us if we were thirsty from the travels here. We drank some tea that she made for us.

Neida took a sip and looked at me in surprise and said, "Mmm, this isn't McDonald's."

I shook my head in disbelief and said, "No, it's better."

Lusamba said, "It's my anti-aging tea. It helps keep me healthy and young."

She asked me to open this huge dusty chest. I pulled up the lid and moved some quilts and found another photo album. We began viewing the pictures. I came upon a picture of a man that looked very familiar. Whoever it was looked a lot like me.

I looked at her and asked, "Who is this?"

She looked at Neida and said, "I don't want you to think bad of me, but that is my first and only true love. He was supposed to be my husband, the father of my children, but one night leaving the festival to return in the morning, he was snatched by the white man and sent to another country. I had love for your great-great-great grandfather Elias but was not in love with him. He loved me with all his heart, and he gave me my children, and for that he will always have a place in my heart. We were snatched together- me, him, and the children. I was able to escape. Elias and my children were shipped to a strange country. That's why I am here."

She retold her story, and I could see the pain in her face and hear it in her voice. She then turned and looked at me. The man I was in love with was your great-great-great grandfather, Marcelo. So she began to tell us of all the great times they had and how she prayed that the enduring love she felt for him she would feel again with them or someone deserving of it. She knew at that very moment her prayer had been answered. She said she was feeling a little tired, and I helped her into her chair. We had to leave, but we convinced her to have a reunion with all of the family the next day. She agreed, gave us long tight hugs, and saw us out. I couldn't believe the gift we'd just been given, it was like we walked back in time. We were so overwhelmed with everything we had just learned. We arrived back to the village. Everyone wanted to know what happened. How had she responded to us? We told them what happened, and they were all excited for us and to celebrate with us the next day. We couldn't stop talking about it the whole way back to the city.

The next day we headed back. Everyone had brought out pots of food, pies, cakes, drinks, and much more. There was a spirit of celebration in the air. We headed down to the bungalow to see about our dear Lusamba. When we got there, we knocked on the door several times. No answer. I pushed the door open with little resistance and we walked in. There she was lying on the bed. I thought she was sleeping, so I went to her and touched her shoulder hoping to awaken her gently. Once I felt her skin, I knew she was no longer with us. I looked at Neida and she was sitting on the bed next to her gently rubbing her legs. I guess all that Lusamba needed was to finally see that her deep love manifested again in us. Through the bloodline which she created.

We went back up and informed the rest that Lusamba had died and as customary we still had a celebration, but it had a different theme. It was her homecoming. The funeral services were like a parade. It was sad and it was beautiful. It had definitely been an ordeal of events over the last several days. After a tearful goodbye, we headed back to the airport. Neida kept saying she was not feeling well. We thought the trip mixed with the heat and the emotions of the last couple of days were taking their toll on her, but when she fainted, we decided to head to the hospital.

We weren't waiting long when the doctor came out to talk to me. I said, "Will she be okay, doc?"

He chuckled and said, "I'm sure she will and you as well."

"What do you mean?

"Congratulations, your wife is pregnant," he said happily as he offered his hand for a hearty handshake.

I was stunned, "What are you talking about? Pregnant?"

He said, "Yes, you are going to be a father, your wife is pregnant."

I was relieved and thankful at the same time. During the funeral I heard an elderly lady say that "a life goes, and a life comes, that's what makes our God so great!"

We were discharged from the hospital with orders to take it slow, remain hydrated, and see a doctor as soon as we got back to the States.

Back at the airport while waiting at the TSA line, we heard a voice calling us, "Neida, Marcel!"

We looked back, and to our surprise we saw Thomas.

"Thomas, Hi! What a coincidence. What are you doing here?"

"I had an emergency back at my company, and I had to catch the next flight out, so here we are again."

Neida said, "Well, if you thought we were interesting the first time, wait till you hear what happened to us!"

Thomas looked at Neida, then back to me and said, "I can't wait to hear all about it. We definitely have some time to kill."

About the Authors

MARSHALL B. CROWDER is a Georgia-born and self-proclaimed country boy. He is an entrepreneur, visionary, and now an author. Writing this book was therapeutic for him, allowing him to use his life and past experiences as a guide to current and future relationships. Along with his writing partner, Luz Eneida, he takes us on a journey of self-discovery, maturity, and accountability.

ABOUT THE AUTHORS

LUZ ENEIDA TORRES calls a lot of places home, having been born in Puerto Rico, raised in Massachusetts, and grown up in California. Being from different places has given her a diverse perspective and worldview. The Wanderer's Enduring Love is her first novel with her fiancé and writting partner. Together they share a love of history and geography and take their readers on a journey much like their own. She currently resides in Little Rock, Arkansas.

Our Motto
"Transforming Life Stories"

Self-Publish Your Book With Us

Our All-Inclusive Self-Publishing Packages
Professional Proofreading & Editing
Interior Design & Cover Design
Manuscript Writing Assistance
100% Royalties & More

For Manuscript Submission or other inquiries:
www.jkenkadepublishing.com
(501) 482-JKEN

Also Available from J. Kenkade Publishing

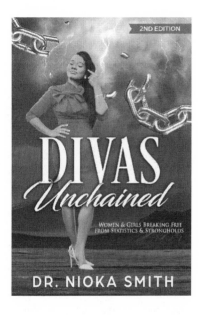

ISBN: 978-1-944486-25-9
Visit www.drniokasmith.com
Author: Dr. Nioka Smith

Sexually abused by her father at the age of 14, pregnant at the age of 17, and a nervous breakdown at the age of 28, Dr. Nioka Smith's painful past almost killed her, until the voice of the Lord guided her into destroying strongholds and reversing Satan's plan for her life. DIVAS Unchained is the powerful chain-breaking reality of the many unfortunate strongholds our women and girls face. Dr. Nioka uses her divine gift to help women and girls break free from destructive life cycles and prosper in all areas of life. Satan has lied to you. It's time to expose his lies. It's time to break free!

Also Available from J. Kenkade Publishing

ISBN: 978-1-944486-48-8
Visit www.jkenkadepublishing.com
Author: Margaret Joanne Rice

Set in the Old South after the Civil War– specifically on a tobacco plantation in Staunton, Virginia– this story revolves around three key groups of people. Plantation owners, plantation workers, and Native Americans play integral roles in this saga. They often intersect and prove necessary for each other to exist in their sociopolitical climate. The conflict in the story involves an ancient Indian folktale about a baby skull hidden on plantation property in a grandfather clock that is shrouded in superstition. This skull is said to have magical powers, and when it disappears, many strange events begin to unfold.

Also Available from J. Kenkade Publishing

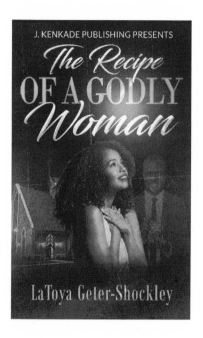

ISBN: 978-1-944486-70-4
Visit www.jkenkadepublishing.com
Author: LaToya Geter-Shockley

A single pastor moves to a segregated town to lead a church deeply rooted in sin. Without knowledge of the sin, he begins to casually date the church clerk. While attempting to bring both sides of the town together, he meets a single mother filled with anger, betrayal, hurt and secrets and finds himself losing sight of God's direction for him. A life-threatening storm destroys the church and the town but opens his heart and leads him to the true woman of God.

Also Available from
J. Kenkade Publishing

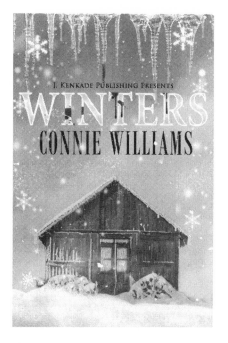

ISBN: 978-1-944486-40-2
Visit www.jkenkadepublishing.com
Author: Connie Williams

Winters is a captivating and passionate Christian suspense novel about a powerful, spiritual family who is anointed and ordained by God Almighty. You will feel love, pain, heartaches, compassion, grace, mercy, suffering, and God's spirit, all in one story. Find out why Winters is about the coldest season of the year in more ways than one. Come and live in the minds and hearts of Stella, Abe, Mr. Perkins, The Langley family, Hattie, Benjamin, and Minnie. So much more awaits you in this powerful Christian suspense novel. Both fiction and nonfiction, Winters will give you a chill like never before.

This page intentionally left blank
by J. Kenkade Publishing

Made in the USA
Las Vegas, NV
12 December 2020